Stranger

By N.M. Catalano

Stranger

Dedication

To my two beautiful daughters. My hope for you is
that you will follow your dreams and always do
what you love. In that you will find peace,
contentment and gratification. It will not always be
easy but it will always be easy for you. I love you
both more than you could ever imagine.

Love does not conquer all.
Sometimes it tries to kill you.
~Elizabeth

Chapter 1

Last night while I was kicked back in my bed, rather than going in for some alone time with my book boyfriend, I decided to flip through a magazine to see what the rest of the world was doing. I came across an article about statistics on ratios of single men to women throughout the US, (it figures I'd still find something about men). It stated that the highest ratio of single women to men is in New York City and the reverse counterpart, men to women, is in San Francisco. Yeah, the gay factor came to mind but it went on to say the primary reason for this is the large tech industry there which makes complete sense. It also listed Seattle, (nope, too wet but I could definitely get into some hot Native American werewolves – I wish), Dallas, (uh, I don't think so, I can't help but think 'All my exes live in Texas'), Denver, (yes, good possibility), and Los Angeles, (I don't know about that). Not that I've completely enlisted in the dating/looking for a man scene. I'm still lurking on the street outside of my enrollment office, so to speak, while I watch the endless line of females go through that revolving door. It's been over two years and I haven't quite completed my preliminaries to join the ranks. Which is why I'm kind of looking forward to tonight.

It's been a shit week. The office has been crazy because of a promotion that's going on which is putting additional demands on all of us. Add to that the regular everyday emergencies and client requests and the network going down on Monday for a few hours. Oh, you can't forget my prima-donna boss who's pregnant with 24/7 morning sickness which makes her such a joy to be around. Mix that all together and stir and you've got one stressed out bunch of ladies. I am so grateful its Friday and it's not often I say it but today I'm ready for a drink. I'm a representative in an office of one of the three major insurance providers in the country. It's really funny when I'm out and a kid just starts singing our jingle out of nowhere; marketing really got that one right. My job is ok. That's the problem. It's just a job and really brings me no self-gratification. And I haven't been 'gratified' in a very long time. That's why Janie convinced me – no, badgered me – into a girls night out. She's one of my only friends and she draws people to her like the ice cream man.

"You need to get out, Elizabeth. When was the last time you got laid?"

She didn't wait for an answer because she already knew it.

"You're ex. I know you said he was the 'the

one' and it was obvious how madly in love you were with him. Hell, you probably still are but it's been two and a half years and you haven't really moved on. I'm pretty sure a lot more happened between the two of you that you didn't tell me and I'm not going to pressure you to but its way past time you got out from under that rock you crawled under and start living again."

Janie is right..so damn right. But what she doesn't know is that I'm afraid. I'm afraid of what could happen if I get involved with anyone.

His name is Santino and people call him 'Sonny'. Yes, there is one similarity to the character in the 'The Godfather': his temper. Except my ex's was a smoldering volcano with bursts of preliminary shooting volcanic rock that culminated in a wrath of an all-consuming thick burning lava which completely devoured and destroyed me each and every time he erupted. It took a long time for me to repair myself when I finally got him to leave. When he unknowingly handed me an opportunity, I seized it with both hands and held his as I led him out the door. An hour after he left I couldn't remember the last time I'd felt peace like that. I'd put him on a plane and he was out of the country and I was free. Or so I'd thought.

He told me very matter-of-factly when we split, or should I say when I attempted to extricate him from being the blood in my veins and the very life-force that infused my existence, that bad things would happen if I was with anyone else. And they did. Some blatant, others seemingly very unrelated. But they did every time, none the less. So, I retreated back into my warm and safe cocoon alone to prevent the devastation I knew would follow and was sure I couldn't handle.

It's finally 5:00 PM on Friday night and I sit at my desk shutting down my computer. I'm going back and forth between looking forward to and dreading meeting Janie and a few of her friends for what could be called happy hour in our quaint little coastal city of Wilmington, NC. Lori, the administrative assistant in the office, is walking by my office on her way out carrying her briefcase with the office laptop in it. Every Monday when I come in and see her emails from the weekend I can't help but automatically roll my eyes. There's more to people than their job and it's sad when they forget that.

She pops her head in and asks, "Are you going to belly dancing this weekend?"

"Nope, girl's night out tonight with an old friend, happy hour, I guess."

"Woohoo, have fun," she smiles playfully, wiggling her eyebrows.

God love her, (as they say here in the south), she's a sweet lady. When I told her about the belly dancing class I had taken she took me on a trip down her memory lane when she used to take a class and how her waist was so tiny back then. She's at least 300 pounds and married to, I think, her second husband whom she met at some country dance.

I chuckle. "We will."

And she adds with a smirk on her face, "Don't do anything I wouldn't do."

It's all I can do not to blurt out, 'There's no worries about that,' but instead I say, "I'll try," laughing. Who knows, maybe those two do get a little crazy, stranger things have happened. Mama could do a little weekend belly dance for papa and they get a little frisky, good for them.

I don't think Wilmington gets enough credit. It's beautiful with its immaculate historic district which, in my opinion, blows Savannah away. The old graceful Victorian homes that line the cobble stone streets with Spanish moss hanging from the huge old oak trees canopying over them are so romantically picturesque. The area has some big companies which makes it attractive for young professionals like PPD and Duke Energy, along with an impressive state university. Also, Wilmington has been dubbed 'Hollywood East' because of the large filming industry here. Ironman III, Stephen King's Under the Dome and Safe Haven are recent and current productions. We have culture, the beaches and lovely safe communities while still holding on to a 'small town feel' because people actually talk to each other here. I was born and raised in New York but have lived here most of my adult life and I look forward to hopefully someday raising children here.

Thankfully I don't live far from my office, only

about fifteen minutes, which comes in handy when I'm running late for work and is more often than I'd care to admit, (typical woman, I know). It's a perfect location within walking distance to everything downtown where restaurants, small galleries, boutiques and the riverfront are always filled with people, great for the favorite pastime of people watching.

When I get home I take a quick hot shower to loosen the tense muscles at my neck and shoulders. Why do women carry all their stress there? The pain can cut like a knife making you so tight that the skin on your scalp feels like it's being pulled down into a tight ball around your neck. As the water washes over my body and transforms me from feeling like a snarling troll to a woman again, my hand slides between my thighs and a wave of heat flashes through me. God, my sexuality has exploded since I've approached my forties, I've gotten much more comfortable in my own skin and my inhibitions have become less and less.

Santino, (I never called him Sonny; I never called any of my exes by their nicknames, their proper names always felt right), had awakened in me things I never knew I yearned for. I never had a vaginal orgasm with him during intercourse but he wouldn't let me go until I came at least three times. He was an amazing lover. And he unleashed the beast within me making me feel like he's ruined me for any other man. No one before him had opened me to passion that hot. But I still held back with him, I could never quite let go. Probably because of all the horrible names he called me and ridiculing things he'd said to me, instilling in me such a bad image of myself that I don't know if I'll ever be able to lose that picture in my head. I guess that's one of my demons I will always have to fight.

But I learned a lot from Santino. We'd talk forever about spiritualism, the paranormal, life and the afterlife. He introduced me to the book The Tibetan Book of Living and Dying and I've got to say it's my favorite. I was reading it on the way back from visiting him once and I missed my connecting flight, I was so engrossed in it. I could only laugh at how ridiculous that was. He opened my eyes to different understandings of life on Earth, possible reasons why we do what we do and why we are the way we are. But as much as I was, and still am, captivated by this amazing man it became too much. And apparently not only for me but for him as well, they say geniuses are the most troubled individuals. I want a normal man to live a normal life with, the whole white picket fence thing, and I finally realized I'd never have that with Santino.

My phone buzzes on the nightstand for the third time with a text from Janie.

Where are you?? You'd BETTER NOT stand me up!

Just leaving, be there in 15 ☺

Feeling pretty good about tonight I go to the bathroom to finish my makeup. A little concealer on my fair complexion, eyeliner doing the cat eye thing on my lids highlighting my hazel eyes, then finish with nude lipstick. I decide on my favorite shoes, the mile high black Jimmy Choo's, because I'm feeling it tonight and I'm only 5'1". It's going to be the black pencil skirt grazing just above my knees over my thigh-high stockings, paired with a white body hugging button up blouse, open just enough to see a hint of cleavage. I have pretty breasts, not big but not too small either. I smooth my long, deep brown hair and pull a little back from my face pinning it to give me some height. I love this conservative look. It doesn't shout 'I'm easy' but rather, 'If you're worth it I might just let you have a taste'. Just because you're on a diet doesn't mean you can't appreciate the tempting delectables of mouth-watering deliciousness of beautiful male morsels.

We're all meeting at The Reel Café downtown which isn't too far from my apartment so I can walk and enjoy the beautiful early October crisp night air. The place is three floors, the ground floor has an outdoor and indoor bar with a large seating area overlooking the sidewalk and another rooftop bar with a DJ while the second floor has a DJ/sports bar. This place is always packed with a variety of people from college kids to the professional crowd. Thank God, I hate college bars, they always stink like puke.

"ELIZABEEEETH!!"

I hear it as I'm just stepping off the sidewalk from across the street. I want to hide but I can't help but laugh as I watch the blonde ponytail swing and arms wave as Janie is jumping up and down like a big kid with a smile spread across her All-American face. She is 30 but she is...not immature but playful. Janie is an occupational therapist and has worked in schools and rehabilitation/retirement centers. Her personality is perfect for her career because it brings a joy of life to the people she's working with. She's a bigger girl, hippy, who loves her college football team but she's just started running marathons and is doing very well. It's so good to see her. Janie lives life and I'm proud she calls me her friend.

I walk up to where she and her other three friends from work are standing, Cathy, Giselle and Amy. Janie's dressed up for her with khakis and a light blue chiffon blouse tied at the neck with flats on her feet. Her friends each have on proper little dresses with modern graphic print that comes to their knees with ballet flats on their feet as well. And then there's me with my 'fuck me' heels. Oh well, I never did quite fit in, it's obvious I'm not southern looking like the misfit of the bunch. I have a European look with high cheek bones, a prominent nose and a bit of almond shaped eyes. Her friends are either married or have a boyfriend and hanging out with Janie is about exciting as their life gets. Mine too, for that matter.

"It's about freakin' time!!" She yells at me, pulling me in to a bear hug around my neck as I give her one right back. We swing side to side smiling, laughing and hugging each other.

"I know, I know. I'm a terrible friend."

"Shut up! You remember Cathy, Giselle and Amy, right?"

"Yeah, yeah, of course, how've you guys been?"

"Great."

"Excellent."

"Fine."

If they're friends of Janie they can't be too stuck up, right?

"So, what's new with you Elizabeth? Any men lately?"

"Jesus, Janie, you know better than that. Besides you would have been the first person I told."

"Well, then you have a lot of catching up to do. Go get a drink and let's get this party started, let's have some fun for once. The guys in here are sooooo hot tonight!"

"What's up with John?" She's had this boyfriend since college I guess who's around ten years older than she is but lives three hours away. Janie's always on the hunt to get laid but I don't know if she ever actually has cheated on him. I've never asked her about it, I don't know how open she would be to tell me. But one night after we'd had some margaritas at a local Mexican restaurant when she was hot for the waiter she told me about a time in college when she'd kissed a girl. I would never have expected that from her and I don't know if it was me who was being shy about the declaration or her. Or if she was fishing for me tell her about any girl on girl action I might have had. That door on the closet of my skeletons is being kept locked up tight.

"He's soooo boring. And he's not here," her dramatics about John are so over the top they're cute.

We all laugh at her.

Take Me To Church starts playing by Hozier, enticing the hormone raging, alcohol loosened bodies filling the bar to find someone to get their freak on with and my body starts to sway to the seductive lyrics.

"I'm gonna get that drink, be right back," I say as I turn to go to the bar.

I stop dead in my tracks. Who. The. Fuck. Is. That? I think my panties just exploded from the gush of wetness from my crotch. The most intense, gorgeous, HOT man I have ever laid eyes on in the flesh is sitting ten feet away. But it's more than this strangers looks that captivates me. It's the raw confidence and primal sensuality he exudes, it's so strong I can feel it from here, pulling me to him with an intense animal magnetism.

Although he's sitting back you can tell he's tall, at least 6', with a sculpted physique but not huge, wearing a crisp white shirt that hugs his torso, leaving a few buttons open at the neck. His arms are lying casually on the armrests and his straight dark hair is rustling in the breeze. He's got the sexiest moustache and beard which he keeps very closely shaved almost like stubble. One of his legs is resting on the other knee in camel colored slacks with expensive Italian shoes. And his deep dark eyes are searing right into me. Instantly another flash of heat shoots up my body and I can feel myself flush like mercury rising in a thermometer. One side of his beautiful mouth lifts into a smirk and I let out the breath I hadn't realized I was holding. There's a glass of scotch held provocatively in his hand, the beads of sweat dripping down its side. I want to be that glass of scotch held intimately in that hand I want all over my body, rolling over his tongue, my taste lingering on his lips. Flowing through the most intimate, private parts of him, heating his veins and exploding in his mind, burning him from his very core. Because I know that is what he would do to me. Movement at his side causes me to notice the smokin' 20 something blonde leaning over his arm to say something close to his ear, almost allowing her voluptuous breasts to spill out all over him from her painted on tiny dress.

Seeing her causes the insecurities I have in myself to come flooding back and the sounds of Janie chattering and the bar around me bring me back from my stupor. I turn my head and move towards the bar knowing my back would be to Mr. Yummy. I grin to myself with satisfaction with the view I've given him because I can feel him eating it with his eyes. I imagine his teeth biting into my cheek and the thought makes my crotch pulse.

When I get back Janie grabs my arm and starts pulling me towards the stairs announcing,

"Common, we're going to find some guys to dance with."

"Oh, noooooo." I whine jokingly.

"Yep, we're all dancing. Move!"

I feel like a little kid being dragged through a grocery store by her pushy mom.

Giselle giggles out loud, "I wonder how many drunks have fallen up these stairs?" I think I really like this girl.

"Not us! We're trained professionals. Don't try this at home, kiddies." Janie, the expert, cracks me up.

The sultry beat of You're So High envelopes us on the dance floor like a lovers caress. I get lost in its seduction and dance as if I'm making love, writhing, swaying and stroking my hips with my hands. I feel someone's hands slide across my waist, flat palms on my stomach, pressing me against the firm body behind me. His mouth comes to my ear and whispers above the loud music.

"You are beautiful."

I don't say anything and just snake my arms around his neck behind mine. His hands are travelling slowly down my hips so I turn in his arms and slide my hands up his chest. He is a pretty young thing with the looks of a hot surfer who happens to know how to move his body and I lose myself in this erotic dance with him.

"I've always loved older women but you are so

damn sexy, beautiful."

I smirk at his comment and decide to play along.

"And what is that you love about older woman?"

"They know what they want," he smiles thinking he's getting laid, pressing his hard-on into me.

"And what is it that we want, lover boy?" I purr at him.

"This, baby." Another poke.

I move my body seductively against his and bring my lips so they're brushing against his ear. "Wrong answer, baby. You want to know what we want?" I slide a finger across his lips, "We want a man who knows what to do with us with this...," then trailing my fingertips down his chest, over his arm, I stroke his fingers, "with these..," then finally I splay my open hand low on his abdomen, "before he takes care of himself. We are not cum receptacles, baby."

Pushing him away I turn, leaving him standing alone on the dance floor. The fool wouldn't know what to do with me if I did go home with him. My steps falter when I see Mr. Yummy and the blonde bimbo standing off to the side and she's disgustingly rubbing her body against him, (bitch). He's watching me with an amused expression on his face and I want to flip him off, it taking all of my restraint not to.

The five of us are standing close together at the first floor bar getting drinks. The breeze is refreshing after dancing and being surrounded by all of those warm bodies because the place has really filled up.

"Elizabeth," Janie turns to me and asks, "have you heard from that nurse?"

I laugh remembering Collin the male nurse. "Yeah, I guess you could say we're still friends. We text or talk on the phone sometimes."

"Tell them about him," turning her attention to the other girls she continues, "you guys gotta hear this."

"Common, Janie, really?" I joke and roll my eyes at her.

"Yes, tell them!"

I let out a heavy sigh and smile. "This guy, I met him on a dating site, really most all the guys I've gone out on dates with I met on a dating site," I laugh to myself. "He's good looking, good job, some beautiful tattoos and all his teeth." They laugh and I lean in closer as they do the same, "then he tells me he's got his penis pierced."

"No way!!" All of their mouths fall open. Except Janie.

Janie is laughing. "Wait...tell them, Elizabeth."

I'm laughing too. "Ok. So, of course I've never seen one like that and he asks me if I want to see it."

Giselle says, (the one with the balls out of the three), "What did it look like?"

"Well, the ring was big enough to fit around my thumb with two balls on the ends. It was pierced right under the hole on the tip just through a little bit of skin so it could move up and down. You know, like door knocker." They're dying of laughter. "I would think that would hurt him when he's having sex but I didn't ask him."

Giselle is all curiosity. "Did you have sex with him?"

"No, but he whipped it out right there in his car. But I will say this, of the three guys I went out with, him I would think about letting my freak come out and play with. If he only kept his mouth shut."

We are all practically rolling on the floor laughing so hard that people are starting to look at us. I look around and not two people away from us is Mr. Yummy. He's got a shit eating grin on his face staring right at me as if he'd heard me. Crap!

Giselle can't get enough. "Who else did you go out with?"

What am I, tonight's reality show?

"Janie, did I tell you about the detective?" I decide I might as well entertain them.

"No, you dated a cop?"

"Yeah, I've always wanted to. This guy is a retired NY detective and we went out about four times. Nice guy, a gentleman except when he said he wanted to buy a fur trimmed pair of handcuffs. That might not have been so bad if his mouth didn't taste like a cavity when I finally let him kiss me."

"Eeewwww," all four say in chorus.

"Tell me about it. But the real winner was the psycho, also from NY, who told me he loved me and needed me on the first date."

"What?! Are you kidding me?!"

"Totally serious. But the best part was when he wanted me to go down on him in his Jaguar parked in front of my house right in his front seats. It was horrible."

"Oh, my God!!!"

"Yeah, so not fun! Dating is definitely not what it's cracked up to be." I take a sip of my wine and glance at Mr. Yummy. He's leaning against the bar, drink in hand, cocking a brow at me. I look at him like, 'What? No one asked you to listen'.

"Common, let's go dance!" We head toward the elevator to go up to the third floor, a couple of glasses too many for the stairs, and I turn my head just before stepping inside. Mr. Yummy and I lock eyes and he lifts his drink slightly at me, smirking. Asshole.

After a few hours and a few dances with guys that are either too young or too old, (I could never quite get into the whole 'cougar' thing, I want a man who knows what he AND his woman want), I'm ready to leave. I've glanced over to Mr. Yummy and his blonde bombshell a few times during the course of the evening while some guys were trying to impress me. A couple of times it looked like he was observing me and would give me that delicious smirk. The kind where you want to lick the contours of his lips and tease the corners of his crooked smile with your tongue.

"Janie, I'm gonna go."

"Nooo! It's so early."

"I've had my quota for the night and I'm not going home with anyone. Besides, I only came out because I just wanted to see you."

"Aw, thanks for coming out. And it's too bad that hottie over there," Janie says with that mischievous smirk on her face looking directly at Mr. Yummy, "is with that bimbo or he'd do you right here. He's been watching you all night."

"Janie! No, he hasn't!"

"Oh, yes he has!" She's smiling like she just told the biggest secret that only she knew.

"Goodnight Janie, goodnight ladies. See you soon."

I slide my purse up on my shoulder and nudge my way through the crowd not even glancing at tonight's fantasy star that will be playing in my mind when I get home.

Its great getting out with Janie every once in a while, it reminds me of how the other half lives. Even when I was younger in my 20's I didn't go out with the girls, I was never part of a clique, not even in school. For most of my adult life I've worked with the public and I know a lot of people but there's only one or two that I would call a true friend. Maybe it's because I'm an introvert at heart or maybe it's because I'm a bitch, I don't think I am but I've been told otherwise. Most nights I curl up with my book and sometimes I think I'd like to find a man again, then there's other times I think my toys are the only things that will satisfy me. Sucky way to live? Maybe, but it's been ok so far.

I walk a block enjoying the fresh night air on my skin, the sky is clear and the stars are absolutely beautiful as the quiet noises of the world float along softly on the breeze. My mind drifts back to *that* man, if there's anyone I would break my celibate streak for, it's him. No one has affected me the way he has in a very long time. It was as if he was seducing me with his eyes, undressing me, making me feel like he was looking right into my soul. I wanted to submerge myself in the depths of him, let him unravel the nice and neat little box that I've packed myself away in and lead me to the cliff of that vortex of ecstasy, and when he finally takes me I'll spiral into that bliss, losing myself within him.

As my mind is completely absorbed in the fantasy I step into the crack of the sidewalk and my spike heel gets stuck almost making me sprawl forward on all fours. Instantly a rock solid arm grabs me around the waist and another hand grips my arm just before I tumble. I wrap my fingers around the arm at my waist and look down at the hand. A tremor goes through me as I instantly recognize that big hand splayed across my stomach, it belongs to that stranger. I feel his warm breath at my neck and he inhales deeply, taking in my scent, making me stiffen and I'm hoping this is real. I slowly turn in his arms, not daring to breathe. And there, inches from my face, is that chest exposed by those few buttons. I check myself to keep my tongue from jutting out to lick his tan skin, wanting to savor his salty taste. God, he smells almost as good as he looks, clean with a hint of male musk and him. My gaze shifts to look up into his face. He's holding my whole body against his rock hard torso as I look into his beautiful dark eyes and notice just a hint of grey speckled in his moustache, beard and at his temples. I feel a twitch against my stomach from his erection and I have to control myself to keep from grinding into it. I know my panties can't hold any more of my wetness from the wicked thoughts I've had of him all night, it'll start running down my legs.

"Thank you," I breathe. I want to bite his chin and run my tongue along his stubble.

We stand there silently searching the other's face, his arms not moving from around me, my hands open wide on his hard chest.

After a moment he says quietly but firmly, "Let's go, Elizabeth," his eyes peering deeply into mine. The invitation is there, not just in his words but also in his eyes. My mind is frantic.

I almost just came.

Chapter 2

My legs are about to give out and my breaths are coming short and fast. This man senses this and holds me more firmly. His hands spread open on my body, one on my lower back just above my ass, the other above that pressing my breasts into his chest as my nipples scream at me to rub them against him while my groin is pulsing and I feel his heat burning into me. I'm torn as three things go through my mind.

First, I'd like to push him against the window of the restaurant we're standing in front of and have my wicked way with him not caring that we'd be on display for everyone inside. Second, I want to drop to my knees and let him have his wicked way with me right there on the sidewalk, whatever he wanted I would do. Third, I fight with the thought I should turn and leave and not look back.

I am so screwed.

We stand like that a few moments that seem like forever. He's waiting patiently for my response and

I'm fighting with the turmoil going through my body and mind. I shift ever so slightly and he steps back fractionally. He feels me relax so he moves, sliding his hand from my back, down my arm and takes my hand, never losing contact with my body or my eyes. My heart is beating so hard that I'm sure he can hear it. He's watching me as if I were a scared little bunny who's waiting for an opportunity to run from this big bad wolf. What he doesn't realize, or maybe he does, is that I want him to skin me alive, cook me over an open fire and suck every tiny piece of meat from my bones then lick my flavors from every one of his fingers when he's done. My inner beast is wide awake and ready to dance.

We walk a block and he's holding my hand, gently circling the top with his thumb. We slow at an immaculate new black BMW 500 series with tinted windows. Neither of us have spoken since those jaw dropping three words. I hear the jingling of keys in his pocket and the lights blink signaling the doors unlocking. Walking me to the passenger door, he opens it and waits for me to slide my pretty ass over the buttery beige soft leather seats. What I'm afraid of is I'll leave a stain because I'm already dripping. He stands there patiently as I hesitate for a second. A glimmer of reassurance crosses his face which allows me to relax a little more and I ease myself onto the seat. It smells like new. Closing my door, he walks across the front of the car and easily folds his perfect 6' body in. Each of his movements, no matter how insignificant, has purpose. When he closes the door, he turns the key and the car hums to life as classical music surrounds us. He sits back and looks at me a moment, studying my face and searching my eyes. What he's looking for, I don't know. Where we're going I have no clue. With whom, I don't even know his name. He's a complete mysterious and sexy stranger and I'm totally intoxicated by him.

I realize our drive will be short when we pull up to the Wilmington Hilton Riverside and stop in front of the valet. There are so many different feelings running through me and so many thoughts going through my mind. I'm nervous, excited, aroused but not scared. I steal a glance at the man sitting next to me and a shiver of anticipation goes up my spine. My mind tells me that I should get out of the car right now, I must be crazy going with him but I sense no threat from him, only attraction and a deep carnal need. Turning to me, he gives me a look that anchors me sending a flash of heat through me. His presence is powerful, strong and commanding. He gets out and the young valet addresses him.

"Good evening, sir."

"Good evening, the penthouse," he says, his voice smooth and commanding, and palms the young guy the keys and a bill.

"Yes, sir."

Striding to my side he opens the door, holding his hand out to me and I look up at him. I see my hunger reflecting back at me in his eyes. How can this smoldering creation of male want me as badly as I want him?

I place my small hand in his, setting one high heeled stiletto on the pavement. A glimpse of the top of my stocking peeks out causing his gaze to move to my ankle, then up the curve of my leg, over my torso and breasts and he squeezes my hand slightly. His perusal stops at my slightly parted lips. My teeth pull in my lower lip as I'm watching him. That smirk pulls up one side of his lips which makes me lower my gaze. He just devoured me with his eyes and I almost self-combusted.

I step out of the car and he places his hand possessively on the small of my back as he guides me through the lobby. He smiles and nods at the desk clerk flashing those straight white teeth, making me smile, too. He catches me and his face lights up. I want to rub myself all over him like a cat, purring deeply as if saying, 'Please pet me'. We stop at the elevators and he pushes the 'up' button. As the doors slide open, he gestures for me to enter first, looking into my eyes almost allowing me the chance to take the out now if I wanted. I step inside and I can almost feel him sigh in relief.

We are alone in the elevator and the electricity between us is palpable, I can almost see it pulling us together. We're so close. His lips crush down on my mouth before his hand wraps around the back of my neck possessively. His kiss is everything, it makes me dizzy, it makes me sweat, it makes my legs tremble. His other hand is cupping my ass while his fingers lift my skirt then slide over my drenched panties, grazing my folds slightly. I moan deeply and melt into him. My hands are in his hair as I'm trying to suck him into the deepest part of me causing a low rumble to come from deep in his chest making me vibrate and I feel it all the way to my sex. My hips grind into him demanding him to give me relief. His fingers only whisper over the soaking mound, teasing me. A sound like a whimper escapes my mouth and he swallows it whispering, "Ssshhh". The bell dings announcing our arrival and being the gentleman that he is he straightens my skirt and makes me presentable before the doors open. My arousal is so intense, I know if he just breathes on my clit I'm going to shatter.

He guides me again with his hand on my back to his door. Stopping in front of it with the key card poised hovering over the slot, searching my face for hesitation, he says quietly with his deep seductive voice, "My name is Marco."

"Of course it is," I reply, the corner of my mouth lifting to a half wry smile.

Could he be anyone else?

Satisfied with my response and seeing the flush of desire over my face and chest after feeling the wetness of my wanting between my thighs, he smirks that incredulous sexy way. He opens the door and, again, waits for me to enter first.

Chapter 3

The penthouse suite is large and elegant for our little city. The couch isn't the typical sofa bed style but a grander piece of furniture with ornate carvings on the dark wood trim. It's covered in heavy cream silk brocade. There is a matching chair, end and coffee table with a partially read NY Times lying scattered on top. A white lily floral arrangement sits on the table at the far end of the room in front of the wall of windows overlooking the Cape Fear River. It matches the woods of the other pieces with curved legs and the chairs are covered in the same rich fabric. On the opposite wall is a huge matching armoire which is closed that must house the TV. On my right is an open door and I glance through it. It's the bedroom with an elegantly dressed king sized bed in creams and chocolates with hints of gunmetal blue topped with tons of throw pillows. The walls are papered in matching colors in a modern motif. I take a few steps into the living area and I can see through the windows a few lights dancing along the black surface of the water of the Cape Fear River from boats drifting silently along.

"Elizabeth."

His voice glides over my skin like a caress, licking me in the most intimate places. I turn slowly as he steps towards me. My breathing is heavy and my heart is pounding.

"Do you trust me?"

I search his eyes as they melt into me and what I find there is hunger, is wanting, and is lust. And I know.

"Yes, I do."

He fills all of my senses when he pulls me close and his mouth consumes mine. His tongue slides along my lips slowly teasing me, demanding to be let in. I open for him and our tongues dance together, licking, tasting, devouring. His flavor is delicious, masculine and sweet. He doesn't just kiss my mouth, he makes loves to it, delicately, passionately, and he makes me ache.

One of his hands is in my hair fisting it, sending sizzling shock waves through me. The other pulls me in tighter and I feel his hardness against my belly. I arch myself molding into him and moan, my sex aching to feel him fill me.

Marco tugs my head back gently with the hair he's holding exposing my neck to him. He buries his face there, nipping me lightly with his teeth then licks the bites he's marked me with. I gasp with the shock of the erotic pleasure.

"From the minute I saw you," Marco whispers into my ear, "I wanted to feel you," kiss, "smell you," nibble, "taste you," lick.

He shifts his body down, sliding his hand over the curve of my ass with a finger trailing between the cheeks until it reaches the hem of my skirt.

"Elizabeth, first I'm going to make you cum with my fingers, feeling that beautiful pussy of yours grasping hard, trying to pull me all the way inside of you," he murmurs between nips and licks on my neck and jaw. I'm panting as my fingers are clawing at his back through his shirt. His fingertips graze the outline of the top of my stocking before continuing their journey up the inside of my thigh and I separate my legs slightly, begging for the contact I need. A light trace along the edge of my panties finally comes to caress the wet lips that wait eagerly below the fabric making me tremble. A grateful heavy breath passes my lips at the needed taunting contact.

"Then I'm going to lay this beautiful body down on that table and I'm going to feast on you until every drop of those sweet juices are mine."

Marco begins to back me up until the backs of my legs hit the coffee table.

"When I think you're finally ready, I'm going to take you to bed and slide my aching cock inside those velvet lips and fuck you."

My body trembles and my nipples are hard at his words, aching for more of his touch. He takes my hand and wraps it around his erection. It's so big I can't get my fingers around it. I feel the throbbing of him in my palm and I imagine how wonderful it's going to feel as he slides it inside of me, the thought making me ache in anticipation. Sliding my hand over the length of him, I flick the tip with my nail. His eyes close and his jaw tenses at my touch pulling another low deep growl from him. Removing my hand, he kisses each finger then my palm.

"If you keep doing that I won't be able to do what I want with you, Elizabeth."

"Please." My voice is shaky and I want to beg, 'Take me now,' but instead I say it with my body pushing into him.

He takes a small step back as his hand glides up my waist moving to stroke the undersides of my breasts with his thumbs while smiling seductively. I am melting into a hot pool of goo from his touch.

"I know, baby. You're mine now and I want to savor all of you completely. This night is ours and tonight nothing else exists but pleasure," his face is a breath from mine.

He makes me believe his words that nothing else exists, nothing can touch us here, not even reality, this is our fantasy meant to be explored.

"You are an incredible woman. When I saw you I could feel that fire inside of you and I wanted to play with it. I'm going to make you explode, Elizabeth. And every time you cum I want you to hear you scream my name."

"Don't play with me," I whisper pressing myself harder into those fingers I want everywhere in and on my body. NOW.

"I'm going to play with you and you will enjoy every minute of it, I promise." He kisses me deeply as his thumbs slide over my hardened nipples.

"Now, I'm going to sit on that couch and I want you to strip for me." Marco's voice is low and raspy showing signs of his fight for self-control. He sits back on the couch in that same sexy, casual and confident way he was at the bar as he undoes a few more buttons on his shirt and I see a light covering of dark hair on his exposed chest.

Holy shit! Can I do this? I'm shaking, not only from nerves but also on fire with the anticipation of the promise of things to come. What if he doesn't like what he sees? I look at the man sitting in front of me watching me, completely seducing me and its evident how turned on he is by the massive hard-on bulging from his pants. But his set jaw and clenched hands say he's trying to keep total control. This takes any doubts away that I might have and gives me the courage to continue. My hand goes to unbutton my cuffs while my hips unknowingly move slightly side to side trying to relieve the aching in my crotch. His focus shifts to watch the movement.

"Stand still. I'll take care of you baby, I promise. Be patient."

I exhale long and slow, biting hard on my lower lip, not breaking contact with his eyes. His look is searing filled with heat and lust while my hands begin to open the trail of buttons at my front. I leave the blouse on and opened, exposing a hint of the white lace bra and rise and fall of the curves of my breasts. I reach behind and slide down the zipper of my skirt, its sound filling the room, and I begin to shimee it down swaying my hips side to side.

"Turn around."

I do as he commands and push the skirt over my hips letting it fall around my ankles. My matching white lace boyshort panties peek out at him just below my blouse with most of my white cheeks completely bare.

"Take your blouse off," his voice is lower, raspier.

This is so erotic, he's got me writhing with only his words.

I let the blouse fall down my back to the floor. And wait. My heart is pounding so hard in my ears it blocks out the sound of my heavy breathing.

"Leave the panties, bra, stockings and shoes on. Now, bend over and pick up your clothes."

I step out of the pool of my skirt keeping my back to Marco and slowly bend over completely opening to him. I wonder if he can see how wet I am from there.

"Turn around." His tone drops a decibel.

I turn slowly and my eyes search him. His fists

are clenched tighter, head bowed with his eyes on me and I can see they're almost black with desire. His tongue slides slowly across his lips and the sight of it makes my mouth open wanting to suck it, my own tongue searching for his.

"Fucking incredibly beautiful woman," he rasps and pushes himself from the couch and towards me in two steps. Taking the clothes from my hand, his mouth lowers to mine, the kiss slow and deliberate, feasting on my mouth. He takes my lower lip between his teeth and bites it gently making me gasp at the slight painful pleasure as he drinks it in.

"I'm going to take you now, Elizabeth." His voice is gravelly with pent-up desire.

"Yes..." Mine low and breathy.

I'm getting high on the drug of his seduction and it is so sweet, so exquisite, seeping through every part of me, I feel it taking me higher and I let go.

Smiling, he cocks one eyebrow and begins to back me towards the couch by my arms, my hands holding his rock solid forearms. Setting my bottom down on the big soft arm of the sofa, his fingers begin a light trail over my shoulders, down my arms, over the exposed parts of my breasts and he follows it with his tongue. My hands tangle in his hair and I lose myself in the back of his neck feasting on the taste and scent of him. He slips a thumb into my bra and pulls it down under my breast, pushing it out. His face is so close I can feel his hot breath on my skin as he traces a circle with the tip of his finger around my already hardened nipple.

"I love your beautiful pink nipples, Elizabeth," he whispers as he lightly twists it between his thumb and forefinger then brings his tongue to flick it. I'm panting and pushing my throbbing sex into the sofa arm. His fingers leave my breast and trail down my stomach while his other hand is on my back. He slides his hand over my panties and palms my sex and sparks explode behind my eyelids.

"Open your legs a little for me, baby," he says against my lips.

I do as he traces the lines of my panties where it meets my thighs, making me want to spread my legs even wider and beg him to fuck me. But he's in control and I'll do whatever he wants. His hand on my back dips below my panties as his pinky teases the crease between my cheeks.

"I need you out of these panties. NOW." The hand on my back pushes me up as he yanks my panties down and off with the other in one swift movement. Without missing a beat his hand is cupping my sex again.

"God, you're so wet for me, Elizabeth." His voice is low and husky. I open my legs farther while his fingers scissor and slide through my wet folds. He circles my clit with his long teasing finger and I'm panting. I have to lock my knees to hold myself rigid, focusing only on the sensations Marco is giving me. My sex is begging to feel him filling me. Answering my need, he slides two fingers inside of me and presses his palm on my clit. All I can do now is watch him, mesmerized, and enjoy the ride.

"So tight, so fucking beautiful," he says deeply against my neck. He's hugging me, one hand on my sex, the other on my back with his pinky buried in the crack of my ass. He's making love to me with his fingers and hands, his fingers sliding in and out, twisting, with a graze of his thumb on my clit. Then he shifts and sets one foot between my legs while my walls are clenching around him. With curved fingers, the tips rub against the front wall while his thumb is flicking my clit. I'm pinned motionless under the onslaught of sensations shooting through me, I'm moving fast towards that orgasmic precipice and he is steering me perfectly.

"Marco...," I whisper, I'm so close.

"Yes, baby?"

"Please...," I moan.

His hand moves from my ass to cover his fingers with my juices then he returns them to my crack and slides one in and out of my cheeks, teasing me. I'm fucking his fingers, grinding myself on them. But what I want is him inside of me and I know he's going to make me wait while he builds my need higher only making the wait so much sweeter. He knows I'm almost there. Pushing his thumb down on my clit, he holds that engorged button firm, rubbing it while his other fingers rub me inside and he pushes me against him from behind.

"Cum for me, baby. Let me hear you scream my name," and his mouth comes down on my exposed breast, flicking his tongue and sucking my raging nipple.

Throwing my head back and arching my back, I grind into all and every part of those fingers and push my breast into his mouth as he takes me over the edge. I scream his name and finally have exquisite release.

I come down with him cradling and caressing my sex and kissing my face, my jaw, and my neck.

"So beautiful, Elizabeth. You're stunning, especially when you cum."

I look at him and a big smile creeps over my face. He wickedly smiles back. What sounds like a growl comes from deep within me, my sex still clenching. I grab him and mold myself into him, hungrily kissing him, pulling his hair, dragging my nails down his back over his shirt. He pulls back and stills, putting one of those drenched digits into his mouth. He knows I want more. My lips part and he pulls it from his mouth and traces my top lip with it, the tip of my tongue catching it.

"Suck it, baby. Taste yourself on me."

I lead his finger into my mouth wrapping it with my tongue and suck it clean.

"Common Elizabeth, I'm hungry," he says low and deep, answering my unspoken request for more.

He takes my hand and leads me to the table, removes the flowers and pulls out the captain's chair. He takes off my bra and bends to place a light kiss on each hardened nipple.

"Undress me. I want to feel your skin on me when I have my face buried in that delicious pussy of yours."

His dirty mouth spikes my passion even higher.

"Shoes and socks first, baby. Kneel down."

I do what he commands. I'd do anything for this demi-god knowing if I was his slave he would do whatever I needed.

As I kneel down he places his hands on my shoulders, stroking the skin there. I remove his shoes and socks and caress his skin with the action. I look into his eyes watching me as I slide my hands up his firm legs and over his bulge to undo his pants. They fall to the floor leaving my eyes level with the huge erection straining under his tight black boxers. I nibble him through the fabric and run my tongue over the wet spot of his precum but he pulls me back.

"No, baby, I want to taste you first."

I sigh heavily and guide his boxers down kissing the skin as it is exposed to me. He kicks the clothing to the side and he sits, taking the same position from before but his clenched fists dangling from the armrests show his need. His erection is standing straight up, red from the blood filling it, its head oozing. I just want to sit on it and slide it deep inside of me.

"Now my shirt."

I lean into him with my breasts lying on his lap

with his erection under me. He's so hard and I feel him twitch under my skin as my fingertips run over his olive complected flesh. I finish undoing the buttons and push the open shirt away from his torso, rubbing my hands over its sculpted definition. I move my hands up to his broad shoulders and push the shirt down his arms feeling the muscles mountaining and braiding into each other. They flex with his fight for composure.

I look up into Marco's eyes and he sees the unasked question in mine. He gives me a hint of a nod and I begin to slither up his long body. I have to feel his skin rubbing against mine.

"Mmmmmmmmmm..." It escapes me before I know it. The hair on his chest is tickling my nipples as I straddle him. His mouth comes down hard on mine and he's lifting me up, holding me by my ass. My soaking wet sex rubs against him as he sets me down on the table with my ass at the edge.

"I can't wait until you cum on my tongue, baby. I want to suck every drop out of you until you feel like I'm sucking your tongue through your beautiful pussy."

"Do it now, Marco, I can't wait," although he's just made me cum my body is humming with need.

"Oh, no, Elizabeth, we're just getting started," he says cradling me and leaning me back onto the table. "Lay back for me, baby. I want you sprawled out like the banquet that you are."

My back is against the cold table, arms lying straight out to the sides, knees bent with my feet resting on the arms of the chair on either side of his large frame and he's leaning over me.

"Just like that, baby, don't move. You're stunning like that. Every part of you is open to me, waiting for me to savor every bit of you."

He sits and takes my legs one at a time, straightening them, nipping and licking the flesh just above my stocking. He rolls the stockings down my legs continuing the trail with his mouth as he goes.

"We can use these somewhere else," he says with a mischievous smile.

His eyes drop to my glistening wetness completely open to him and he licks his lips. Shifting his gaze to my eyes he lifts one of my feet to his mouth and kisses then licks the arch. I gasp as he grins wickedly, giving this same attention to each toe. He repeats the same agonizing torture on the other foot making me relaxed and frenzied at the same time.

He takes my stockings that were hanging on the arm of the chair and comes to stand next to my head as I watch the perfection of his body move. I can't help focusing on his engorged penis standing at attention as if saluting me. He leans down close to my face laying an open hand on my stomach. My back arches up off the table and he kisses me lightly, tracing my lips, my mouth and my teeth with his tongue.

"Do you trust me, Elizabeth?"

I search his face silently peering into his deep dark eyes.

"Yes."

"I would like you to let me do something for you."

I wait for his request as my heart rate accelerates.

"I want you to let me bring you the most pleasure I can. I want you to concentrate on feeling everything I do to you. To help me do that I want you to let me blindfold you...with these." He takes the stockings and traces them up the length of my body from my feet, over my legs, across my sex making me jump, and over each nipple. The whisper of the touch is intense.

I stare back into his eyes. He's patient waiting for my answer. Anticipation and desire course through me making me delirious. I nod slightly and whisper, "Ok."

He kisses my swollen lips deeply. "Thank you, baby."

He takes the stockings and holds them above my face sliding them between each hand, looking into my face for signs of fear or hesitation. "If you can't handle anymore and you want me to stop, just say stop, Elizabeth. But just know we stop completely. Nothing else. Do you understand?"

I stare up at him as he holds the stockings very still over my face. Waiting. The sight of those stockings become an aphrodisiac, the latent desire to be dominated, to submit myself completely to a man I know is worthy, comes out of that closet I've tried to keep locked up and my body bows inwardly with sultry surrender.

"I understand." The words are so quiet I don't know if he hears me.

Marco immediately smiles knowing that I have given myself to him, at least for tonight, to do what he knows I need and want.

"You've made me very happy. Ok, lift your head up a little, baby, and close your eyes."

And everything goes black. All of my other senses are immediately heightened. I hear the scrape of fabric as Marco quickly ties the nylon in place. The hardness of the table is defined under my body and if I flinch I feel its coolness where it hasn't been warmed by my body heat. Body heat. I am so hot. I feel the air rasp in and out of me. His finger traces my lips. I smell myself on him and I lick my lips in anticipation. His mouth is on mine capturing my tongue, sucking it into his warm mouth. His hands are on my arms and he begins to gently guide them straight over my head holding them firmly.

Marcos mouth is close to my ear, so close that I can feel his warm breath before he whispers, "Keep your arms over your head like this, love, hold on to the table." My body is stretched jutting my breasts up as if they are calling to him and he answers the call taking an aroused hardened nipple between his fingers and strokes the tip.

"Your body is my playground tonight, Elizabeth,

and I'm going to play with it now," the heat in his voice is erotic and sultry and I melt in his hands.

I can't speak, I am incapable of answering him with words but my body responds as mouth falls open, my heart skips and heat flashes through me and everything within me clenches in need.

He begins the seductive play on me with absolute focused attention beginning with my breasts, tracing the curves of them then turning to my nipples first with just his one finger then two. His mouth finally captures them teasing them with his lips then only his tongue bringing me to the point of madness and on the verge of a climax. My hips begin to move writhing in need. His touch is leading me closer to erotic oblivion, a place in which I'm afraid I will never want to leave.

"Stay still, Elizabeth. Feel me. Don't move or I'll stop and we'll have to start over."

A sound like a whimper leaves me quietly. I can feel the breath from his mouth so close to my ear now.

"Sshh, baby. Trust me. Just let yourself go with the pleasure," he whispers to me licking and nibbling my ear. And with that, the heavy curtain of restraint falls away as I let go completely.

"Yes," I reply panting.

I inhale deeply as the pinky on my stomach begins to tease my mound and I struggle to hold still. The waves of sensation are carrying me out further into this space of mindlessness, one where nothing else exists. His hand travels downward bringing his fingers to slide through my wet folds as one enters me and circles. My focus is fixed on that finger taking me higher. I'm being pulled from my body with each of his movements as if within and without myself. He lifts my leg to his shoulder, his tongue on my legs, licking and kissing my calves. He stills. The sound of our heavy breathing is the only thing I hear.

"Your pussy is so beautiful with its pink lips begging to be kissed. So wet..." and he nestles a finger between my cheeks moving upwards gathering my juices up over my folds to my clit and circling it. "You're dripping. It's all I can do not to bury my cock in you right now, Elizabeth. Next time I'm going to take you like an animal."

"Oh, God, Marco, yes...." My whole body is rigid imagining his beautiful length plunging into me.

"I know, baby, I know." His hands leave me and I hear the rip of paper. He places both of my feet on the arms of the chair and holds my legs open.

"Keep your legs open for me just like this baby, don't move." I feel so completely open and exposed to him, it's frightening and erotic at the same time. Then he's on me beginning the journey up my legs with kisses, licks and nibbles. When he gets to that crease at the top of my thighs he strokes it with a long lick and I think I'm going to lose it. One hand lies just above my mound and pushes back, exposing my swollen clit. The contrasting cool air hitting it feels intense. His tongue takes another long lick over my wet lips then dips inside and pulls them into his mouth, sucking them in.

"Aaaarghh!"

Flicking my clit with the tip of his tongue, he swirls it around that tiny bundle of electric shocks. He plunges deep into my hole and begins to fuck me with his mouth. He's feasting on me, lapping me up with such precise devotion and it's hedonistic. His hand presses down harder on my abdomen holding me still. Back and forth from tonguing me to licking me and flicking my clit, he never gives me enough to push me over the edge, keeping me poised there hovering ready to fall. So close, so fucking close, he knows exactly what he's doing to me.

"Please, Marco...," I beg.

He moans while he's sucking on me and I feel the vibration penetrate me, intensifying the sensations. Two fingers clamp down and pinch my clit rubbing together as his tongue lavishes my sex, licking, suckling and plunging deeply inside of me. Overcome, I fall, soaring, arms out wide like wings, as I unravel into bliss. The release is slow and sensual and I glide with it, moaning his name out loud.

Suddenly his mouth is gone and I feel him at my entrance.

"YEEESSS!!" and he plunges into me as his balls slap my ass. He's so magnificently big filling me completely, exactly what I was yearning for.

N.M. CATALANO

"YES, YES, YES!" I scream as my walls grab hold of him, milking, pulling him in as my orgasm builds again.

In one swift movement he lifts me up still buried deep inside of me, pulling the blindfold off, carrying me to the bed, sliding out, turning me over with my ass in the air face down, and plunges into me again. One hand is holding onto my hip and the other slides through my folds and rubs my clit. My orgasm is cresting again and I'm slamming back on him, circling my hips grinding my clit into his hand as he's pounding into me.

"Fuck me Elizabeth," he growls plunging in and out, grinding circles into me.

I'm milking him with my orgasm pulling his release from him. His fingers leave my clit and I feel one wet with my juices circling my ass.

"Yes, Marco, please...," I beg as I continue to grind into him as he slips his finger in. "Oh God, Marco!" I moan as we're pounding into each other. My orgasm explodes again. HARD. He buries himself deep inside of me completely, pulling my hips back onto him as I feel him tense, tightly holding me to him.

"Fuck, Elizabeth!!!" and I feel his cock twitching inside me as he cums releasing his passion into me, thrusting long and deep.

We collapse on to the bed with him inside of me still hard. I feel him twitching with the aftershocks of his orgasm as I continue spasming and milking him. My back is to his front and he's brushing his lips along my neck and shoulders, pulling me in closer as I push down on him.

I realize I haven't seen all of him yet while he's explored every inch of me. I move so he slides out and I turn to face him, my hands on his chest as he's stroking the length of my body. Staring into each other's eyes, the air shifts and I feel the stirring of his erection against me.

"I want to look at you, Marco," I whisper.

He studies my lips then his mouth is on mine, his tongue caressing me tenderly. He pulls me closer to mold me against his naked body.

"Anything for you, baby."

He lifts himself off the bed and removes the condom and throws it in the trash. Every inch of his body is finely sculpted. His ass is perfect with those indentations on his cheeks that you want to rub your face against. His sculpted broad back tapers down to a defined waist. But what my eyes focus on is the breathtaking dragon tattoo. It starts at his left shoulder blade and winds its way down to his waist. The reds and blues are so striking I can't help but reach out and touch it as I get up on my knees to run my fingers along the lines. He flexes and the dragon moves as if it's coming to life.

"It's beautiful," I say quietly and bend to lightly kiss it.

He looks over his shoulder at me and says, "You're like a dragon, Elizabeth, with that fire raging in you."

"Are you sure you didn't wake the sleeping the beast?" I ask cocking one eyebrow at him.

"That was the plan, I possessed it." He smiles wickedly, turning and taking me in a deep kiss.

"Now sleep, baby, because I'm gonna wake it again in the morning."

I lie down and he pulls the soft covers over me and kisses me lightly on the forehead.

"I'm going to order breakfast for us then come and join you."

I smile contentedly and settle into the big pillow. The beast in me is totally satisfied and is curled at her master's feet. Maybe he did tame me.

I slowly wake up to the sounds of my moans as my body arches up in need. My legs are wide open riding the fingers that are working their magic on my sex. Two fingers are inside of me and Marco's thumb is teasing my already swollen clit. The sensations are intensified by my sleep state and I feel like I'm gliding in bliss.

Marco turns me to my side not removing his hand from me. His other arm is under me reaching over onto my breasts, pulling me close to his front. He pulls one leg up bending it at the knee and slides his rock hard erection along my wet lips coating it with my juices. It feels so good. I'm still floating in that sleep haze as I reach between my legs and guide the head of his cock to the entrance of my hole. I slide myself along it, loving how it teases me. His fingers return to my clit as he slides just the head in. I grind my ass into him and I feel his growl on my back. One hand is flicking my nipples, the other my clit. I push my ass down on him and bury him deeply in me, filling me as his fingers take my clit between them and I shatter into fiery pieces.

"Marco...," it comes out as a deep moan.

I push down on him and grind into his fingers and cock as the orgasm rips through me riding the waves of my release. He's still holding my clit between his fingers, working it between them, prolonging my orgasm as he begins to slide in and out of me long and deep as my walls are pulsing on him demanding his orgasm. He tenses and buries his face in my neck and I can feel him jerking inside of me.

"Yes, Elizabeth!" His voice is so deep and gravelly.

And I feel him cumming. He stills with every inch of him in me. I reach between my legs and take hold of his balls and lightly scrape my nails along the contracted wrinkled skin. He spasms as he lets out a loud growl. We lie still, wrapped in each other, coming down. Our heavy breathing is the only sound we hear.

The knock on the door pulls us from our languor. Marco turns my face to him and kisses me deeply.

"Take a shower if you'd like, love. That's our breakfast. I had them bring some things up for you earlier." His thoughtfulness touches me and makes me smile.

"Thank you, I will. I'll be out in a little bit." I stretch feeling completely content with a big smile spread across my face. I couldn't stop grinning even if I wanted to.

I admire him as he gets up and pulls on a pair of jeans as he turns to look at me one more time and smiles before he leaves the bedroom, pulling the door closed behind him.

The bathroom is elegant and enormous with white marble floors and counters with a separate Jacuzzi tub and walk-in shower. I look in the mirror at my reflection expecting to see a different woman. I gasp at the morning smeared makeup face staring back at me and I can't help but moan thinking, 'Oh my God, how could he stand to look at me like this.' I just want to bury myself in a hole.

I notice there are two sets of toiletries on the counter, his and hers, and I can't resist the urge to pick up each one of Marco's personal items to get a different glimpse of the real man. These aren't your corner neighborhood drugstore brands and I can tell he's got very specific tastes. I open each individually inhaling the scents as they send tremors through my body eliciting the image of his body against mine. Afraid that I'm taking too long, I turn on the shower and place the items for me to bathe with inside as a part of me doesn't want to wash him off of me. I can't believe that this is me and I'm here in a beautiful strangers bathroom and we've just had a night and morning of the best sex I've ever had.

After I've showered and scrubbed the homeless looking lady from my face and dried my hair I dress and meet Marco in the living area. He's sitting peacefully on the couch reading todays New York Times dressed in only those jeans with his feet propped up on the coffee table. He hears me and turns to look and a smile slowly lifts his lips. I stand feeling a little embarrassed because I don't have any makeup on, I call it my war paint because you go out in the world to battle every day, and it makes me feel a little vulnerable.

"You're even more beautiful now, Elizabeth." The words are so soft and genuine.

I can feel the blush creep across my cheeks as my eyes lower to the floor. I don't know how to act because it's been so long since I've been alone with a man like this after a night of intimacy and I feel so very vulnerable. My usual confidence has left the building without leaving instructions and I feel like I'm on stage and I've forgotten my lines.

"Thank you."

He stands and holds his hand out to me. I take it and we walk to the breakfast table laid out with several plates covered in silver domes with two pots and two cups and saucers.

"Come, let's have breakfast. I'm sure you're starved, I know I am."

He removes the covers off the plates revealing a banquet enough for four people. There are Belgian waffles, scrambled eggs, whole wheat toast, fresh fruit, sausages, bacon, Canadian ham and yogurt. In the thermal pitchers there's coffee and hot water with tea bags sitting to the side in a variety of flavors.

"My God, Marco, this is enough food for a party, do you always eat like this?" I can't hide my surprise with the spread of all the food.

He laughs while he holds a chair for me to sit down and says, "No, but I didn't know what you liked so I got a little of everything."

During breakfast our conversation is light and relaxed as if we'd known each other forever. When we finish he sits back in his chair with an amused smile on his face.

I squirm and begin to feel slightly embarrassed again knowing whatever he's thinking is about me.

"What?" I ask smiling nervously.

"So, even though I don't have my cock pierced or didn't have any fur trimmed handcuffs and, God, I hope I didn't taste like a cavity, thank you for trusting me."

I bury my face in my hands knowing I am beet red by the heat flooding my face as I'm turning red again, I've lost count of how many times that has happened with him.

"Oh, no, you *did* hear!" I moan and this time it's not from lust.

He howls in laughter. "I couldn't help it. Did you really date those guys?"

I look up at him laughing, "Yes!"

He's still laughing and I can't help but laugh with him. The sounds trail off as he's studying me. "Good, that kept you for me."

The air is sucked from my lungs as I stare back at him not really knowing what to say or think about that.

"Well, I had to fill my time somehow, you know," I try to make light of it.

He's like a mystery I want to figure out. Looking at him I tilt my head to the side trying to determine what kind of a man he is. It appears that he's not a player, he is not the type to pick up a quick piece of ass and I believe he's definitely not looking for a wife, I can't quite put my finger on what this man is all about.

"Tell me, Marco, is that how you find all of your playthings?" I ask smiling at him hoping to get a feel of what he is.

He seems to think about my question as his finger lightly strokes his lip not answering me immediately.

"No." That's it, that's all he says and I'm left with more questions and absolutely no answers.

My gaze fixes on his hand wrapped loosely around his empty coffee cup. It's fine china, which I find a little unusual for a hotel, with a silver pattern around the rim with the Hilton emblem. The delicateness of the porcelain is accentuated against his big hand but not foreign to his touch. One of his fingers begins to trace slow circles along the rim with the finesse of a lover caressing naked flesh. The intimate sight of his stroking finger brings me to that erotic place he had taken me to last night with only his fingers. A ripple of desire begins to flow through me again and I feel my face begin to flush. I raise my eyes to his and I know he can see the effect on me with that innocent movement.

"Maybe I should go now" I say quietly, not wanting things to get awkward. But maybe what I really want is to leave him with him still wanting me.

His face becomes expressionless. Did I insult him?

He hesitates, maybe to dissuade me, but says, "I'll drive you. Give me a couple of minutes to get dressed." He insists and I give in.

"Thank you. I'll just sit here and try to forget you heard all of that."

He stops on his way to bathroom and bends to brush his lips against mine. "Don't be embarrassed, Elizabeth, we all have our stories."

When we reach my place he gets out and opens my door for me. He takes my hand as we walk to my front door and he pulls me into an embrace, holding me close for a long moment. I don't know what to say now. What do you say to someone after a night and morning like that? 'Thanks for the mind blowing sex. Have a nice life.'

Instead he takes the lead and he says smiling while still holding me, "Do something special for yourself today, Elizabeth. And think of me when you do."

Fuck. Why does he have to be so great?

"Don't work too hard, Marco. And don't chew them up and spit them out," is all I can think of. I want to kick myself thinking that was stupid.

He throws his head back and laughs. It's a great sound.

"I'll try, baby, for you."

I have to leave fast before I beg him to take me back to his hotel room or I invite him in. I kiss him lightly on those luscious lips one more time lingering just a bit longer savoring the taste, feel and smell of him. Then I turn and walk towards the door not looking back.

I'm still high from the unbelievable past twelve hours. I can't get over the fact that I actually allowed myself to just leave with a complete stranger and let him do whatever he wanted with me. But to be perfectly honest, I was a damn lucky woman. I have never been made loved to like that. He explored all of me, guided me to pleasure with mastery, taking control knowing when I was ready to fly then carrying me on the winds as I dove. I can't help but giggle out loud hugging myself each time a wave of desire hits me, bringing me right back to Marco playing my body like that sweet BMW of his, driving me where he wanted me and pushing those buttons to make each part of me come alive.

I decide to do exactly what Marco suggested and do something special for myself. Why not? I deserve it. I have felt bad about myself for way too long, existing and not really living. So, first I'm going out for a walk just to enjoy being alive. I want to fill myself with more. I want to open my arms wide and breathe deeply and experience as many sensations as I can as if I was blindfolded like last night. We desensitize ourselves to the small subtle beauties of the world and let the tiny miracles of life go unnoticed. As they say, you gotta stop and smell the roses. And I want to do just that because they are smelling exceptionally beautiful today.

The day is lovely, the sky a clear blue with not a cloud in sight. My mood is slow and languid, just a continuation of the past hours erotic dance. When I got home I'd put on a robe getting out of my dirty stay out clothes. I change into black yoga pants, a form fitting white T and a blue hoodie for my walk. I grab a bottle of water out of the fridge and head out.

The smell of autumn billows around me on the breeze from the dry leaves in their little whirl pools on the ground going round and round. I hear the scratching of the squirrels stocking up on nuts getting ready for the colder months ahead. As I get closer to Market St. the sweet smell of waffles hits me. Kilwins Ice Cream Shoppe has the best waffle cones ever. It's like the witches house made of candy and I'm Gretel and it's luring me in. I turn the corner and go in for my cookies and cream fix, I can't resist the temptation.

The rest of the evening I spend pampering. It's been years since I've done this and I promise myself I'm going to put me first again. I deep condition my hair and mask my face before a long hot bath. Next is a manicure and pedicure, nude on my fingernails and red on my feet. I finish off my self-indulgent night with the movie P.S. I Love You. It's all about allowing yourself to live again and that's exactly how I feel, I feel like I've been brought back to life. All the while Marco's ghost is my ever present companion with thoughts of him filling me. The memories of his smell, his touch, his taste are still so fresh on my mind and body.

Lying in bed with my eyes closed my thoughts drift through everything that has happened to me until this point. It's like I'm looking at the highlights of a movie on mute clicking frame by frame. Woman is drawn to a man. Click. Woman worships that man. Click. Man appears to adore woman. Click. Man opens woman's passion. Click. Woman gives up everything for that man. Click. Man beats woman completely, emotionally and physically. Click. Woman is alone and withdrawn. Click. Mesmerizing stranger appears. Click. Stranger pulls woman in. Click. Woman let's go to desire. Click. Woman is alive again... Next frame please. Nothing. What's the next frame going to be? I don't know and I shiver with a tinge of fear from things I'd thought I'd buried deep and I push them back. It's up to me to decide if I'm going to continue to hide because of Santino's threats or will I allow myself to live my life fully and do whatever I have to in order to do that.

Chapter 4

Monday morning. Ugh. Here's a little message for you:

"Dear Monday, fuck you."

9:30 and there's already a shitload of calls to make, quotes to catch up on and follow-ups to do. And I can't get my mind off that mysterious man, Marco, who controlled my body and took me to places I'd hungered for never realizing they were real. He blew into my life like a hurricane sweeping me in for hours then leaving me washed on the shore under the bright sunshine as the waves lapped lovingly at my skin as I wondered if it had all been a dream. My breath catches and my body reacts to the memories. It definitely wasn't a dream.

Another ripple of fear threatens to bubble to the surface and I push it back again. 'No, there's no way Santino can find out about him. There's no trail, no emails, nothing that can link me to him. No one knows but us.' I relax content with carrying these memories in my soul until I'm old and grey when I can pull them out and remember that passionate night of sweet abandonment.

I jump as my phone rings. I see it's Carol who is the senior rep in the office and I smile. I love that woman. She's the most endearing person I've ever met. Carol is the epitome of good things in small packages, strong and badass, she's former military and she even keeps a small gun in her desk. Yet she's kind and gentle.

"Yes?"

"Miss Sue Whiggins, get in here now."

I laugh out loud at the joke. She and I play at that old Carol Burnett skit. I'm Carol Burnett as the secretary, because I've got the 'junk in the trunk' as Carol says, and she's Tim Conway as the boss.

I walk across the hall to her office and sit in the chair across from her. There's a lull in the traffic and calls coming in to the office right now so we take a five minute break to have a little girl time.

"So, what's up with you, Elizabeth?" She leans over her desk leering at me scrunching her eyes like she's about to interrogate me and I feel the blush heat my face. Damn, I can't hide anything from her.

"Nothing, why?"

"Don't give me that crap. What's up?"

I let out a heavy sigh and look away trying to decide if I should tell her or make up something. I know I look like the kid whose eaten every last cookie from the cookie jar smiling at my secret crime while a few stray crumbs are still on my mouth.

I look back at her smiling. "I met someone."

"It's about friggin' time. Who, when, where?" Her face beams with excitement.

"His name is Marco at happy hour Friday night." I try to keep my excitement low.

"And...?"

I hesitate. I'm about to bust. To hell with it, she's safe.

I lean in towards her as a wicked grin spreads across my face and I lower my voice. "The sex was in-fucking-credible."

"Holy shit! I'm so happy for you. When are you going to see him again?"

My face drops. She doesn't know about my past only that I was married and I prefer to keep it that way.

"I'm not. It was just one mind-blowing night. I don't even know his last name or what he does or even if he lives here." I pause. "And that's how I want it."

She studies me trying to read anything else on my face. Her hand reaches out and holds mine as her expression softens with caring.

"Honey, this is only a new beginning for you. Finally you opened yourself up. You deserve to be happy. I'm so glad he reached in and pulled you back to life."

"It's not quite that easy but, hey, maybe. Who knows, right?" I attempt to sound like I don't care and that it was no big deal but she can see right through me.

Unexpected tears threaten to fall from my eyes and I can't reply because of the knot in my throat. Carol looks at me with questions. Thankfully the phone rings and snaps us out of our deep little moment. I silently sigh in relief, a reprieve from the questioning I was sure Carol was going to begin and the emotional reaction I was just falling into.

I laugh, "Back to work," and I get up to return to my office grateful for once for the office phone ringing.

Tuesday's are kind of neglected. Monday gets a beating because it's the beginning of the week, Wednesday is humpday and everyone loves it because it's half way to Friday, Thursday is the 'almost there' day, and Friday, well, we know what Friday is.

Sitting at my desk mid-morning with a cup of decaf french vanilla coffee I get a text from Elsie, a girl I met while working on the Safe Haven film, I worked in accounting and she worked in wardrobe. Elsie is a free spirit, a little gypsy mixed with faerie, with a couple of beautiful tattoos and short blue black hair and she is the sweetest girl I've met in a long time. She moved to the East coast when the filming industry began picking up here again. We've hung out a few times while she was in between movie projects while she was back in Wilmington after Safe Haven wrapped. I smile because I'm genuinely happy to hear from her.

Hiya Liz! Back in Wilmington for a little while, how've you been? ☺

Great Elsie! How are things with you?

Great! Got a Halloween party to go to, you wanna come?

A slight feeling of apprehension simmers at the back of my mind. I'm not much of a socializer and these sorts of things always make me uncomfortable because I feel like a fish out of water at them.

Maybe, is it with some of the crew?

Yeah, why don't you meet me at my place when you get out and we can talk about it.

Sounds good, you know if I go you're gonna have to help me out with a costume.

Lol, don't worry, girlfriend, I've got you totally taken care of already ;) See you later.

Lol, see you about 5:30, have I told you lately how you are just the friggin' best!

I know, just have your ass here by 5:30 so I don't have to hunt you down!

A Halloween party, I'm excited! I've never been to one, only to the clubs, so this is something new for me. My mind starts thinking of possible costume ideas as I say a silent prayer of gratitude that Elsie is a master at costuming and wardrobe and I have to keep myself from squealing out loud in childish excitement. This could be really fun and I think that maybe life has a way of taking you where you need to go even if you don't know where that is. I think Tuesday's just got pretty cool.

I see Elsie's VW Beetle parked on the street outside of her apartment building as I'm walking up the block. She lives in one of the few true multi-story apartment buildings in Wilmington. This one in particular is special because it was used in the movie Blue Velvet and when I look at it I get a creepy feeling up my spine. I decided to go home first to change then walkver to her place since she doesn't live far from me. I buzz her apartment on the intercom box that has seen better days outside of the building so she can let me up.

Yes? comes Elsie's grainy voice from the old silver panel on the red brick wall.

"Open up, little girl, I have some candy for you." I can't help but chuckle

You are crazy! Hahahaha, common up!

Bzzzzzzzzzzz. And I push the door open before the annoying noise stops and I have to call her again. I pause at the elevator wondering if this prehistoric looking contraption will get me to her third floor any faster than my feet will and as I do I hear it coming down, the door opens and out comes a beautiful Barbie looking college age girl. She looks me up and down then turns her head jutting her nose up in the air. Damn, I must look exceptionally good for her to act like that. Sometimes you can't help but give people exactly what they ask for.

"Well, sweetie, no need to be like that, one day you're going to grow up and maybe be a beautiful woman too. Have a nice night." I see her steps falter slightly as she gets to the door but she exits quickly without turning. I probably shouldn't have done that. Who the hell am I kidding, she deserved it, the stuck up princess.

When I get to the third floor, tiny Elsie is leaning against her open door waiting for me. She's got an oversized NY Yankees t-shirt hanging off her shoulder and cut-off denim shorts with flip flops on her pretty feet with black polish on her little toes. Her short raven hair is brushed over one eye with long bangs with some spiking up haloing her pretty face and head, she looks like the most adorable little Emo pixy with her dazzling smile.

"You are so lucky you didn't stand me up, Elizabeth. I'd have come and dragged your ass here kicking and screaming. Come here and give me some love!" Elsie lovingly threatens me.

"No doubt, Elsie, I am totally afraid of you, you scare the shit out of me," and I pull her in for a great big bear hug. She is the only female adult that I know that is shorter than I am but she's solid as a rock also, being part angel and part devil.

"Come in Miss 9 – 5. Looking good, girl," she beams at me and although I haven't known her for very long, two years really, she is a very good friend. This is one person you should not judge by her cover. She is extremely committed to her talent, doesn't drink except an occasional glass of wine, doesn't smoke or do drugs, but she has a mouth like a truck driver and won't hesitate to punch you in the face if you deserve it. I've seen her do it at the wrap party for Safe Haven when one of the camera guys grabbed her ass and made some lewd insinuations at her. She turned around, smiled sweetly at him then pulled back and cocked him, laying him right out.

"Thanks, Elsie, you too, you get more beautiful every time I see you."

"Aw, thank you, maybe I can be as beautiful as you one day."

I laugh and turn to ask her, "Speaking of which, do you know the Barbie blonde that lives in your building?"

"Yeah, I can't stand that bitch, and I let her know it one day after I got back from a project."

"I just ran into her in the lobby downstairs and did the same thing." I can't contain my pleased surprise when I answer her.

"You're kidding me, very cool. What happened?" Her smile is from ear to ear.

"She looked me up and down and gave me a dirty look. I thought she must be jealous so I just reassured her that one day when she becomes a woman she might be beautiful too."

"You did not?! That is so perfect, that is exactly why I love you!"

"Yes, I did, there is no need to be like that. And no need to take it either."

"Common, sit down, would you like some tea?"

"Love some, do you have chamomile?" I ask as I enter the living area.

"Does a bear shit in the woods?" Her reply comes to me from over her shoulder as she turns to put the kettle on and reaches for the mismatched antique tea set, sugar bowl, creamer and tea leaf holder, this girl loves her tea time and she does it right.

Elsie's home matches her completely. It is a cross between a Gypsy wagon and a Victorian boudoir with feminine touches of lace and floral with splashes of vibrant satins of reds with gold trim and tassles. I take a seat on the antique sofa done in deep purple velvet with carved wood trim, a large black steamer trunk sits in front of it as a coffee table. The dark wood end table has an antique brass lamp with a cream colored shade with clear beaded trim that looks like crystals. I reach over to turn it on and the warm fuzzy lighting immediately casts a small circle of romantic haze in the room. Elsie comes in and sets a tray down set with the tea service on the trunk and joins me on the couch.

"So, what's new with you, Miss Elizabeth?" She fills both of our cups with tea and continues, "Cream and sugar?" She must have lived during the Victorian era. I can see her now in her big bouffant dress entertaining her suitor.

"Yes, please, one sugar. Not much really, did you just finish a project?" The image of us sitting down like this would probably look a bit surreal if anyone were to come in but this is what we do and it's great.

"Yeah, I was working on an HBO series in Atlanta, a pilot, I don't know if I'd want to go back and do it though, if it takes off. I'd like to get onto Sleepy Hollow here, I know a couple of people that are working it, and there's Witches of East End as well besides Under the Dome. So, I'm putting my fingers in and seeing what they'll come back with." She looks at me curiously and asks, "Why did you get out of the business?"

I sigh and think back to two years ago when we were working twelve to fourteen hour days before I answer. "My dad was sick. He passed away last year. I decided after that I needed to get back into a field that was a little more stable, although I wouldn't mind the travelling and getting paid to do it. But I need to start settling down again, I won't be in my 30's for too much longer." I smile at her, she is both young and old at the same time, an old soul in a wild body, and it's beautiful.

"I understand. Hell, I would enjoy putting down roots and designing my own things with a lovely little boutique. I think that would be wonderful."

Her eyes take on a dreamy expression as she imagines it and she looks so content.

"I'm sure when the time is right for that you'll know it. I have no doubt there's nothing that you couldn't do, Elsie."

This is what I enjoy most about spending time with her. Neither one of us have any baggage with each other, I have no past, no family. She, to me, is just this fantastic eccentric, talented young woman with her whole future open wide to her. And she's grounded while still having her head in the clouds and I admire her for that.

"Which is exactly why we're going to talk about the Halloween party. I had some ideas for costumes that are absolutely perfect for you, Elizabeth." She looks so excited.

I can't help but laugh at her enthusiasm but my sensible side is makes me reign her in. "First we need to talk about that, tell me about the party before I agree to go. I'm not going to some wild and crazy thing."

She laughs so hard she has to put her tea cup down so she doesn't spill it all over. "You know I'm not like that. No, it is an industry gig, and I know you'll recognize some people from Safe Haven but there will be more professionals there besides grips and crew. It's on Friday, Halloween night at the Wilmington Hilton Riverside, the studio rented out some space."

Now I have to put my cup down not believing

what she just told me. Elsie looks at me and she can tell that something is up.

"What is it, Liz?"

I look at her and just smile as I remember walking through the lobby of the Hilton with Marco the other night, and the feel of his hand on my back sends tremors through my body making me catch my breath at the image in my mind. The memories are beginning to feel like a distant dream, the only thing keeping them a reality is my body's reaction to them.

"I was just there the other night." I can't hide the smile that creeps across my face.

"Oh, you dirty little thing, tell me everything!" She inches closer to me with excitement written all over her face.

I laugh, "It's no big deal really, I met someone at The Reel Café Friday night and he was staying there."

"Don't give me that shit, last time we were together you were coming out of your marriage and had practically secluded yourself on a deserted island. Now spill it!"

"Okay," I give in, "it was the most amazing one night stand I've ever had." I tell her how he followed me out and how I went with him not even knowing his name. And about the night of erotic pleasure he gave to me, the look of sensual satisfaction still lingering in my eyes.

"But I've got to say, El, to me it seemed like sex

to this man is an art form that he's mastered and the female body is the canvas that he uses to create his masterpiece. Or a musician and I was his instrument that he played perfectly knowing just where and how to touch me." I envision in my mind his hands, fingers, mouth, tongue, teeth on my body putting together the symphony of my desire.

"Damn, this man must be something else for you to give in to him, Elizabeth."

"He was the most stunning man I have ever seen, but it was more than his looks, it was him, the raw sexuality, the power, the confidence, everything about him that just oozed from him. I wanted to drown in all of it." I look her in the eyes and say, "And I did. I would do it again, all of it and more."

"Fuck, if you ever see him again, ask him if he's got a brother. I want to take a swim in that ocean of ecstasy." Elsie fans herself and I can see her face flush just from my words. We look at each other laughing at our obviously spiking libidos.

"Now, let's talk about costumes, Elizabeth," her eyes become animated as she begins to lead me into her world and we talk about them for an hour before I leave and I find myself looking forward to something in the future for the first time in a long while.

Lunchtime Wednesday I'm feeling pretty good. I've written some nice policies and have a few more prospects that look very promising. I'm sitting at my desk starving and wondering what I'm going to have to eat for lunch while talking to a client on the phone when my phone alerts me with a text message. I decide to wait until I hang up because I'm already distracted with my hunger and the ramblings of the person on the other end of the line. I need to pay attention to the details the client is giving me. After a long while of trying to keep him focused just on the information that I need to prepare his quotes rather than his life story I hang up and check the message. The guy was going off on tangents from his past, to his move down here, the ice storms we had last year, to his neighbors, anything that entered his mind he talked to me about and I had to listen and tactfully steer him back. Sometimes I wonder if the conversations we have with some of our clients are the only interactions with another person they have during that day, it's the least I can do to show them some kindness and attention.

"Oh, my God!" I can't contain my surprise and Carol pops her head in as she's heading out the door.

"What is it, bad news?"

I look up at her with a stunned expression on my face still holding my phone.

"You know Mr. One Nightstand from Friday?"

Her eyebrows pop up to her hairline and her jaw hits the floor.

"Marco?"

"Yeah..."

I hand her the phone to let her read the message because I still can't believe it myself.

Hi baby, I miss you. I got your number off your phone.

She looks at me and I just shrug my shoulders like, 'I don't know'. She goes back to reading.

Tonight, dinner 6:00 at Aubriana's. I'll pick you up. Marco

Carol looks at me and I stare back, both of us shocked.

"Are you going?"

I think about it.

"Yeah, I guess." And we both burst out laughing.

"Damn, girl, you must not have been so bad yourself!"

"Shut up!" I laugh at her, turning red. I wear my emotions so plainly all over my face there's nothing I can hide, I'm such an open book.

"I'm just saying...," she throws over her shoulder on her way out the door.

I send him a short message.

Well, well, I suppose I can make it. ☺ ~ Elizabeth

The phone dings immediately with a reply.

Hahaha, I would be very grateful. ☺ Yours,

Marco

How grateful? ~ Expectantly, Elizabeth

On my knees grateful, baby. Sincerely, Marco

You're very good on your knees. ~ Appreciatively, Elizabeth

You have no idea yet, love. Promising, Marco

Holy shit! I might need to go home and change my panties. I don't think they'll make it through the rest of the day.

The rest of the afternoon drags by probably because I keep checking the time every five minutes, I'm been so excited I couldn't sit still and I've been smiling for no reason at all. Maybe that's not true, maybe it was because visions of Marco keep dancing through my head and all of the glorious things he did to me. Its 4:45 and I sit contemplating on whether or not to send Carol an IM. 'Is it necessary?' Well, it's better to be overly cautious now than be sorry about it later.' I can't take any chances, I know I shouldn't see him again anyway but I can't resist him, I yearn for him so badly it hurts.

PLEASE don't tell anyone.

Don't worry, sweetie, you're safe with me.

☺Thanks

I get the feeling Carol knows more about me than I think she does.

I'm already sweating and a nervous wreck before I even leave the office at 5:00. And I still have an hour until I'm face to face with the stranger I think is God's gift to women's bodies. I say a quiet thank you that I can see him again although I'm fighting with myself, one side saying stay away and the other side getting her prettiest lingerie out of storage. It's so glaringly obvious which one won.

I love my home. It's a two bedroom attached section of a historic mansion that was built around the turn of the 20th century. The high ceilings with huge windows make the interior spaces feel majestic. The original hardwood floors have been redone in a deep dark brown with the worn pathways throughout making it very homey. I kept the walls painted white and covered them in black framed family photos. There is an original fireplace that was closed off long ago so I've filled it with candles. The furnishings are muted white, cream, black and brown with pops of color in accessories. My couch is invitingly big and overstuffed with a set of antique captain's chairs on each side which I redid in cream velvet fabric with the wood in ebony stain and lacquered. The dining table is also antique with the same wood refinishing and matching cream velvet covering on the chairs. The kitchen has stainless steel appliances with the breakfast bar and kitchen countertops in black granite. The cabinets are also white with brushed silver pulls. It's feels like a refuge more than an apartment to me.

I rush in at 5:15 frantic trying to decide on what I'm going to wear. I wore my hair pulled back in a tight ponytail today, great day to pick that hairstyle, so there isn't much else I can do with it now. The ponytail will have to stay but I can pull up a little on the top of my head for height and to dress it up a little bit more. I decide on a brown jersey-knit body hugging dress that's scooped low in the front with brown leather stiletto boots and a thin brown leather belt around the waist. Perfect, not too dressy but sexy. I jump in the shower hoping I don't have to shave. At 6:00 on the dot as I'm putting on the last touches of makeup the doorbell rings and I jump.

"Get a grip." I repeat the mantra over and over as I go to answer the door.

He takes my breath away the instant I open the door, I'd almost forgotten how beautiful his chiseled face is. He's dressed in perfectly fitted jeans and a snug black cotton T with black Italian driving shoes on his long feet. His dark hair is combed back and still damp from a shower. And he smells divine. This man definitely has a natural sexy sophistication and confidence that would seduce any man or woman, straight or gay.

"Well, well, if it isn't Mr. James Bond, man of mystery," I smirk.

He laughs deeply and takes a step through the door closing it behind him then pulls me close.

"Well, Elizabeth, I couldn't give up all of my little secrets now, could I? You would get bored with me so quickly then."

"Marco, I don't think there's a boring bone in your body."

"And certainly not in yours. You look absolutely beautiful. And thanks for meeting me on such short notice."

I roll my eyes playfully. "Well, I had to move some things around so I could fit you in but I forgive you this time."

"And I completely intend to show you how much I appreciate it but right now we have reservations. Are you ready to go?"

"Yes, just let me grab my bag."

I turn to go but he pulls me back to him.

"Wait, baby. I've been dying to kiss you since you walked away from me the other day." And just that little bit sends a wave of heat through my body. Both of his arms wrap all the way around me holding me tightly to him as mine reach up around his neck. The kiss is long and deep and full of hunger. We finally come up for air and he rests his forehead against mine still holding me to him.

"Hi," he breathes smiling deliciously at me.

"Hi," and I melt at his look.

"I missed you, Elizabeth." His arms tighten around me and my heart jumps.

I hesitate. What do I say? I can't tell him what I really feel. 'I missed you too, you've been the only thing on my mind. I can't wait to feel your body against mine again.' I can see he notices my hesitation as different emotions passing quickly through his eyes.

"We're going to be late for the reservation," I say quietly.   It's all I can manage.

"Yes, you're right. Let's go, I want to show you off."

A slight ripple of alarm goes through me. 'There's nothing to worry about it,' I tell myself and push it aside.

"So, tell me Mr. Bond, why didn't you *ask* me for my number?"

He cocks an eyebrow pausing. "I wasn't sure if you'd give it to me and I don't take no for an answer. I wanted to see you again, Elizabeth." He looks at me as if to challenge his reply. I don't and just let it go. There is no reason for us to get any further than this and I think there could be so much in his answer, I can't help but feel happy about it and I force myself not to overanalyze things.

He leads me down the walkway with his hand going around my shoulders as mine automatically goes around his waist, my thumb hooking through his belt loop, our actions so natural, fitting together comfortably and intimately as if we'd done this a million times.

"Would you like to walk?"

It's dusk and the air is cool and fresh, a night that makes you feel alive. The sunset is a vibrant orange red glowing against the clouds as the wind pushes them along and the moon is a whisper through the darkening blue sky.

"Yes, it's beautiful out."

"Yes, it is," he quietly answers, his face so close to my profile I feel the contrasting warmth of his breath on my skin and I turn my face to his smiling, his lips brushing mine. It's been so long since I've felt truly appreciated and wanted by a man and I feel beautiful with him. I can't help it as a little piece of my guards fall away.

We arrive at the restaurant and the maître d asks if we have reservations.

"Yes, Kastanopoulis."

I didn't want to know any more information about him but at the same time I'm dying to know all of his little secrets and everything that makes him tick. What his favorite foods are, if he's a beach or a mountain person, does he like to read or watch tv?

Aubriana's is a lovely little fine dining restaurant while still having a casual feel with exposed brick and is decorated in deep rich colors. When we enter there is a woman's voice filling the air singing with so much emotion and lust as if she's seducing her lover with her words. The dining room is fairly full for the middle of the week and I glance around to see if there is anyone that I recognize. Not seeing anyone I know I let out a small breath of relief.

We are led to an intimate table in the corner with Marco's hand possessively on my lower back sending electric tremors through me. It makes me feel like he's claiming me, like I belong to him. That is what I miss from a relationship, belonging to the man I love. He holds my chair as I sit down then seats himself next to me. His knee rests against mine under the table as his hand gently takes mine in his on top.

I can tell the waitress has fallen under Marco's spell because she's blushing and fidgeting standing at the side of our table. He appears not to notice, politely giving her his full attention. Typically someone with his obvious status would be pretentious and cocky. Not him. This man is definitely not a dick. Marco orders the brown sugar cured Scottish Salmon skillet roasted with baby spinach, toasted country ham and black eyed peas vinaigrette. I get the slow roasted organic Springer Mountain Chicken with creamy mashed potatoes, English peas, roasted pearl onions and sherried chicken jus lie. I decline the wine because I don't want to have a headache tomorrow but I really think it's because I want to be able to process every little detail of tonight not wanting to forget a thing. We eat from each other's plates and feed the other tastes from our forks when something is just too good saying things like, 'You've got to try this.' During our meal Marco always keeps contact with my body either with his leg against mine, his hand holding mine, or wiping the corner of my mouth. Our conversation is light and flows naturally like we are long time lovers knowing all of our intimate secrets, all the little things that make us happy and those things which get on each other's nerves.

When the lovestruck waitress clears our plates we sit back in our chairs relaxed, gazing at each other. Marco's arm is across the back of my chair and he's lightly stroking me with his fingertips as the underlying lust that has been simmering between us all evening begins to heat up. I lean in closer to him placing my elbow on the table and rest my chin in my palm looking into his eyes.

"So, Greek, huh?"

He laughs lightly and nods his head.

"Yes, Greek and Italian. My father is Greek and my mother Italian. They owned a Greek diner in upstate New York while I was growing up. That was my first job, of course, and I hated it. They worked all the time and it killed me to see how much it took from them. After I graduated high school I went to college in the city at NYU and studied business. I loved Washington Square Park. All the talented people there on the weekends was amazing."

I laugh. "I know. I went to FIT, (Fashion Institute of Technology), and lived on West 4th Street next to the Pink Pussycat Boutique. I used to hang out there all the time."

"You're kidding me?"

"Totally serious."

"And was it the park or that adult store you hung out at all the time, Elizabeth?" His tone has changed to a sultry, dark, challenging lick across my skin

"The park," my body reacts to his voice more than his words.

"Did you shop there?"

"No, I was too young."

"Would you now?" His eyes take on a hint of something, what, I don't know, a challenge maybe.

I think about the question just a moment visualizing myself blindfolded with Marco using toys on me.

"Yes."

A seductive smile lifts his lips. And he hesitates as if he's thinking about my answer.

"And are you a fashion designer?" His demeanor shifts very slightly, hardly noticeable but I feel it more than I see it.

I laugh. "No. I worked for an accessories designer when I lived in the city. Back then I thought I wanted to be in that world. But now I think it's haughty and shallow."

"Yeah, I agree with you. Don't hate me for what I'm about to tell you but while I was at NYU someone approached me in Washington Square Park and asked me if I wanted to do some modeling so I took him up on it. I was a kid and thought, 'Partying, beautiful women, it's a man's dream'. It paid ok but it didn't satisfy me. I finished school then moved to Florida and got into what I'm doing now. I..........."

I raise my finger to his lips, shushing him.

"Don't. Let's just be the two people that we are in this moment." I move in closer, our faces just inches from the other.

He looks searchingly into my eyes and I know he's trying to figure out what I mean by that.

"I think that *you* are the woman of mystery, Ms..............?"

I can't help but smile at his insinuation.

"DiStefano. My name is Elizabeth DiStefano."

A big grin curves his luscious lips.

"My Italian beauty." His mouth comes down on mine consuming it as his hand wraps around the back of my neck holding me close. We kiss as if we were alone, not caring that we're in a room full of people because right now it's just us.

There is a shuffling noise that pulls us out of our intimate bubble and we look up to find the waitress standing a foot or so from the table blushing a deep scarlet unable to look us in the face and Marco begins to chuckle. I squeeze his thigh under the table to scold him.

"Um, would you care for dessert, sir?" He looks at me with one brow up questioningly.

"I have cookies and cream ice cream at home." I smile suggestively at him.

His eyes deepen at the suggestion as a grin lifts his lips and he says, "My favorite. Just the check please."

It just got really hot in here.

The walk back to my apartment is perfect, the stars fill the clear night sky and I can hear owls hooting in the distance as horse drawn black and white carriages stroll past giving a hint of slower times. We hold each other close, his arm tight around my shoulder, mine around his waist as he's telling me how much he likes the charm of Wilmington. He says he was surprised to find the growth of the area and how it still is able to retain its warmth. I tell him the little bit that I know about the area and what it is that I love here. I love that it has so much to offer in an intimate way, I love that people still talk to each other and strangers nod and smile their hellos in passing, I love that I have watched children grow up and they still remember me telling me about the time they remember the most.

When we arrive at my door the street is quiet as he takes the keys from me and he unlocks the door, stepping aside for me to enter first, a gentleman is always a gentleman no matter how dirty they are in private. The door closes behind us in the darkness and solitude of the room and he immediately pulls me into his arms, devouring me in his kiss with his hands all over my body.

"This is where I've wanted you all night, Elizabeth," he whispers against my neck.

"It's all I've thought about all week, Marco," my words come out as a pant.

"Common. Let's go have some ice cream," with a wicked look in his eyes he takes my hand and leads me to the kitchen with the only lights illuminating our way coming in through the windows.

"You have a beautiful place, Elizabeth. It feels very comforting." Stopping, he leans me against the end of the breakfast bar.

"Thank you. I love it," I reply high with arousal, I'm surprised that I can even speak coherent words.

"It shows." His eyes narrow at me. Our mouths are having one conversation while our bodies are having another. "Don't move, baby." He says low and firm, desire obvious on his face.

After turning on only the nightlight above the stove he goes to the freezer, pulls out the container then looks through the drawers to find a spoon and takes it out. He comes and stands in front of me, removes the lid and spoons out some of the sweet cream then puts the spoon to his mouth and slowly wraps his tongue under it with his upper lip on top. He's staring into my eyes as I watch his mouth intently imagining it on my body.

"Mmmm, delicious. Would you like some?" His voice is so sultry it strokes my skin.

My eyes still on his mouth I can barely answer, "Yes, please."

Marco slowly touches my lips with the spoon and I have to tongue a taste. He pulls the spoon from my mouth and brings his mouth to mine, sucking the cream from my tongue.

"Mmmm," he moans in my mouth. "But I think it can taste even better." He puts the spoon in the container and sets it on a chair. Leaning in he lays both hands on the counter at my sides bringing his mouth close to my ear and whispers, "I'm going to eat the ice cream off of you, Elizabeth." My jaw drops. And he smiles seductively satisfied with my reaction.

He slides one hand up my arm to my ponytail and holds it lightly as his mouth grazes my ear. "You have beautiful hair, baby." Wrapping my hair around his fist he pulls my head back slightly giving him access to my neck. He nibbles and sucks me there inhaling deeply. "I love how you smell. I lied back in bed after you left the other day so I could smell you again remembering every delicious part of you."

"And what did you think of?" I pant.

"What I wanted to do to you next time. Now, I need you naked." And his hands undo my belt then reach down and grab the hem of my dress pulling it off. He devours my body with his eyes. Kissing me passionately, he removes my bra, cups my breasts and thumbs my hard nipples. His mouth lowers to each nipple sucking and flicking the tips with his tongue. His hands slide down the sides of my body as he crouches in front of me and begins to unzip my boots, taking each one off, kissing and caressing my legs and slides my panties down. I grab handfuls of his hair and push his face into me. All of my clothes and shoes are in a pile to the side. He has his hands on my hips and nips my pubic bone hooking his tongue to my clit sending shock waves through me. I push myself into his mouth holding on to his 'just fucked' looking hair and tug. He stands holding the backs of my thighs and lifts me on to him, wrapping my legs around his waist as my arms go around his neck. He sets me on the counter as I'm grinding into him trying to satisfy the ache he's made in me. I am just about to become desert.

He guides me down onto the stone surface. "Lie back, Baby, I want to enjoy you," he commands sealing his words with a deep kiss.

Taking the ice cream container in one hand he begins to tantalize one breast, sucking, biting and licking the tip. The shock of cold ice cream suddenly on my nipple sends waves of heat to my sex followed by his hot mouth immediately sucking it off. I push it hard into his mouth while my ass writhes into the hard surface beneath me. He does the same to the other. The coldness feels like fire. He continues, filling my belly button with it then licks it off burying his tongue in the crevice and I feel it straight to my core. I will never look at ice cream the same way again.

"Oh, God, Marco...."

Grabbing my hips, he pulls me down so my ass is at the edge of the counter and guides my legs around his neck. I want to shove his face in there and ride his mouth hard and fast. He begins to lap up my juices, taking my clit between his lips and sucks it sliding one finger slowly inside of me as he does.

"God, Elizabeth, you're so wet. I love how you

want me." His finger is thrusting and twisting in and out of me. I want more, I want him inside me filling me up. I clasp down on it clenching it in my inner walls. His tongue flicks my clit before his lips grab it and suck it in. He goes back and forth between flicking and sucking. He's killing me, keeping me right there and he knows it. He pulls his mouth off, his finger still inside of me as it thrusts and turns. Then coldness hits my clit making my back jump off the counter.

"Aaahhhhhhhh!"

Two fingers are thrusting inside me now, twisting, curving and rubbing the front of me as his mouth comes down and takes hold of my clit covered in ice cream between his teeth. He swallows the cream taking my button of electricity between his hot lips and sucks. I immediately cum, spasming, writhing, holding him tight between my thighs, as I'm pulling his hair and screaming his name. Fucking me with his fingers as his lips hold my clit, he laps up my juices as I come down.

"Wow, that was...."

"We're not finished yet, baby," he says, his voice low and rough and he pulls me to him wrapping my legs and arms around him. "I've got to be inside of you."

He lifts me to him with hunger in his kiss and carries me to my room.

My bedroom is like a place where a sheik would keep his harem, done in deep reds and golds with a black wrought iron headboard with only a small lamp glowing on the nightstand. I want him to use me like a harem girl and do very naughty things to me. He places me gently on the bed and begins to undress as I enjoy the presents he unwraps with each piece of his clothing.

He's looking down at me and I feel the need I see in his eyes. "You are so sexy, Elizabeth."

"You make me feel that way, Marco."

"Good, I want you to know what you do to me."

His shirt is off and he's unbuttoning his pants, letting them fall and I look hungrily at his erection straining against his black boxers. I take in all of him with my eyes burning him to my memory, tucking it away in my secret place so I can take it out when I want to feel him close. Pushing his boxers to the floor he bends to take something out of his pants. He rips open the condom packet and slides it over his huge erection. Climbing up the bed to me I wrap myself around him once again. We kiss and stroke each other fiercely as if we're starved, devouring each other with our kisses, licks, sucks and caresses, feverishly rolling all over the bed. He pulls me so I'm on top of him.

"Ride me, Elizabeth. I want to watch you make love to me." There is nothing more that I want right at this moment than that. I want to make it last, pulling him inside of me and ride him into mindlessness.

I sit straddling him and lift up as he reaches down and places himself at my entrance. I love the way the tip of him feels pressing against me as I slide the entrance of my wetness around him, teasing myself, spiking our need.

"Oh, God, Elizabeth..." His head goes back, eyes closing and I lower my mouth to run my tongue from that soft spot under his throat all the way up to his mouth. I want to feel him, taste him, smell him, suck him into me completely.

I push myself down filling myself with him in one movement.

"Oh, yes, Marco, you feel so good," I moan.

He pulls my face down again to kiss him. My hands on his chest, I begin the dance of our lovemaking, sliding the length of his beautiful cock in and out of me and rubbing myself against him. I almost hear the steady rhythm of the music in my head, beginning to build, pulling me with it. I lean back and stroke his balls behind me, fondling them in my hands. His pushes up into me, throwing his head back, his mouth opening. His hands are caressing me, my breasts, gliding all over my body. I can feel my orgasm growing, my movements becoming more deliberate. He sits up with his arms wrapping around my waist and circles my ass with his legs and I hold his face and kiss him hungrily. Holding me he begins to circle my hips around skin to skin.

"Yes, Marco..." My back arches thrusting my breasts into him as I dance on his lap. He's grinding my clit into him, his mouth pulling my breast in as he's pumping into me.

"Yes, yes, yes..." I move with him, the

crescendo of the music is building in my head and in my core. I put my hands on his legs and increase my movements on him, pushing harder, grinding up and down more and more. He can feel me tightening on him and I feel him twitching inside of me.

"Now, Marco! Now!" And he thrusts deeper and grinds harder pulling me down on him again and again.

"Fuck me, Elizabeth! Use me, take what you want!" and he slams himself into me as deep as he can and holds me there. He tenses as I feel him spasming inside of me with his orgasm. One hand goes to one nipple and twists it as he takes the other into his mouth, teeth closing and tongue flicking on it. Grinding my throbbing clit against him with his mouth and fingers tantalizing my aching nipples, I explode.

He falls back on the bed pulling me with him holding me tightly to him. We lay like that, my head to his chest listening to his pounding heart as his hands stroke the length of my body.

He rolls me so we are on our sides face to face.

"I can't get enough of you, Elizabeth."

"Me too, Marco."

He breathes in deeply and squeezes me tight. "Let me clean the stickiness of the ice cream off of you. And I'm sorry but I think I'm going to have to get you another container. That one's probably melted."

"Oh, I think it was worth it."

"I'm very glad you think so," his smile is sinful as his lips brush mine. "Be right back."

He gets up and goes to the bathroom. I watch as the muscles of his body flex with each of his movements making the dragon stretch. It's such a beautiful sight and it makes me sigh with appreciation. A second later I hear running water then he's back with a wash cloth.

"Here, let me clean you, baby."

"I think you did an excellent job of getting it off of me already."

"Best ice cream I've ever had." He laughs.

He takes the cloth and gently wipes the sticky residue off my breasts, stomach and sex. He's smiling as he cares for me and I marvel at how he can be so rough and so gentle at the same time. He returns the towel to the bathroom and is still semi hard when he climbs back into bed with me. He's looking at me with that look every woman wants, one of desire and adoration, the one that says he thinks you are the most beautiful woman he has ever seen. And my heart grows, almost bursting with the sheer enormity of it.

"What would you like to have in the morning?"

The question takes me off guard because I hadn't thought of tomorrow, I'm only relishing the now. "Just some breakfast tea and you."

"Is that all?" he says with a smirk.

Wriggling up to him I visualize waking up with him again and smile to myself with the thoughts, "There really isn't anything else you haven't taken care of already, Mr. Kastanopoulis."

"There are a lot of things I can think of but we'll take it one thing at a time, Miss DiStefano." His smile is deliciously wicked.

My heart flutters. I don't know if its apprehension or happiness but I think it's both as I let myself fantasize about the decadent things he could do to my body.

"Well then, that certainly will give me something to think about."

Chuckling, he places a light kiss on my forehead and says quietly, "Now sleep, baby. I want to shower with you in the morning which will take a little longer than you're used to."

The thought of him naked and wet in the shower, our bodies sliding against each other, makes my eyes widen, suddenly waking up early will be something I'll look forward to.

"Ok, but first I need to use the restroom." I say a little embarrassed.

"Ok." He is laughing softly.

I get up to leave not bothering to put anything on but worried a little bit about anything jiggling as I walk. Santino's words about my fat are a faint background threatening to squash my afterglow.

"And by the way, you've got a beautiful ass and

back. I love watching you."

"I knew you were watching it in the bar the other night," I say looking over my shoulder and see Marcos appreciative stare. Santino's insults are immediately ignored.

"I know you did," he laughs.

I come back and slide up to him and he spoons me close, his arm wraps around my waist and he kisses my neck then my shoulder and my lips. Warmth and emotion envelope me and I feel safe, it's a wonderful feeling.

"Good night, Elizabeth. Sweet dreams, beautiful."

"Good night, Marco. I will with you here." Did I just say that?

"That's what I want, baby."

I snuggle in close, squeezing into him. I have a big smile on my face and the last thing I remember is feeling his breath on my skin and his heartbeat on my back and I'm filled with contentment as I let sleep take me.

The early morning sun streaming in through the windows wakes me. I forgot to close the curtains last night. Groggily I remember why and I reach my arm across the bed to touch Marco's firm body. But it's empty. My eyes open to confirm that as I hear sounds coming from the other room. I get up and notice his shirt and jeans are folded on my dresser and his shoes are placed neatly in front of it. I go over and pull his shirt over my head and think to myself that I love the smell of him on me as my heart beats a little harder. I go to the bathroom to freshen up first to make sure that homeless lady hasn't come back for a visit this morning.

I walk into the kitchen and see a cup of tea waiting for me and Marco drop dead hot in his boxers leaning against the counter checking his phone with a cup of coffee sitting beside him. One foot is crossed over the other and his hair is a glorious mess. Lifting his head, his face breaks into a smile. I notice he's folded my clothes and put them on a chair and set my boots to the side as well. The ice cream container is nowhere to be found. Holy shit, he picks up too.

"Good morning baby, nice shirt, it suits you," his arms open as I walk into them.

"Good morning, and thank you, perfect length. And nice boxers." I ogle at how they hang low on his hips showing that delectable happy trail. I want to trace a line with my tongue all way down to where it ends, like the pot of gold at the end of the rainbow.

"Thanks but I would have to disagree on the shirt." He wraps his arms around me tightly and kisses me.

"I didn't know what you took in your tea," he says huskily as his fingers graze lightly across my cheek tucking a stray strand of hair behind my ear.

"One sugar and milk." My voice is suddenly

low and breathy.

"Drink it fast so we have time for our shower, baby." I can feel him harden against me as my wetness grows between my thighs.

My bathroom is nostalgic in feel with black and white subway tiles with a claw foot tub, separate shower and a pedestal sink. Marco holds my hand while he reaches in and turns the water on and checks the temperature. When he's satisfied he turns to me and pulls his shirt over my head.

"I like me on you, Elizabeth," he whispers as his hands slide down my naked body.

"I do too, Marco. You feel good," I say quietly with as my lips feather along his shoulder.

Staring into my eyes he removes his shorts. I noticed a pack of condoms sitting on the sink when we came in so I take a chance.

"Is there any reason I should know of that you would need that?" I say looking at the condoms. "There isn't any for me." I'm hoping he tells me what I want to hear.

"None what so ever, baby. There is nothing more I want than having nothing between us so I can feel that velvet skin inside of you. Common." And he leads me into the shower, his erection rock hard.

The hot water envelopes us in a waterfall as we kiss hungrily beneath it. His skin is beautiful like satin caramel glistening with water droplets cascading from him.

"Me first," I say as I reach for the shampoo. I lather his hair and love how it feels in my hands, so thick and silky, as I feed the strands through my fingers. I replace the shampoo in my hand with bodywash and squirt some into my palm. I begin my exploration of his body at his neck then over his large shoulders, down his arms, over his back paying close attention to my dragon, (yes, it's mine because it is me on him), then his tight ass and I resist the urge to bend down to bite it. I stroke his skin memorizing the contours of his body under my hands like a blind person reading braille. His skin feels like velvet under my touch and I want to wrap myself up in him. I move to the front and begin at his neck again, I go under his arms, over his chest outlining the curves and plains of it and I stop to play with his nipples. When I see his reaction to how I'm touching him with his jaw tensing it fuels my fire. I move slowly down his abdomen over his taut stomach and his hands clench at his sides in anticipation of where I'm going. I work the lather up in his hair circling the base of his cock. I reach between his legs and cup his heavy balls moving them around in my palm. My hand slides back as I run a finger between his cheeks.

"Fuck, Elizabeth." His eyes darken intensely watching me but not moving.

I bring both my hands to his shaft circling them in opposite directions. Moving one hand to cup his balls again I slide the other up to the head of his cock and slide a finger just under the rim. I want to tease him, build his desire until he can't think straight. I move to circle the head, my hand gliding over it then down his length. As I'm pumping his shaft and fondling his balls his hands clamp down firmly on my wrists.

"If I don't stop you, you're going to make me cum and I want to be buried inside you when I do. My turn now, baby," his voice is deep and full of pent up desire, just like his balls. He will not give up control.

Taking the bodywash from me and replacing it with shampoo he begins the most sensual scalp massage I've ever had. My back is to him as he's rubbing my head, neck and shoulders. It's heaven. He rinses then fingers some conditioner through my hair while he plays with it. Now it's time for my body and I'm already on fire before he's even begun. Starting at my feet lifting each one before moving up my legs his touch is light but firm. He moves to caress my ass cheeks, running his fingertips along the bottom curves of each then gently sliding a soapy finger between them as I push back against him. Continuing up my back with his touch becoming more firm, he massages my tight muscles. I'm turning into jello under his expert hands and the hot water and it's divine. He lifts both my arms stroking them with the soap and holds both wrists over my head in one of his big hands and places them on the shower wall. His free hand gently encircles my throat as his body presses firmly against me. He continues to move down my chest, over each breast tracing their curves and stopping to thumb my nipples. I'm rubbing my ass up and down his erection, feeling my cheeks hugging him. His hand continues over the entirety of my torso not leaving any inch of flesh untouched. By the time he reaches my soaking wet sex I'm moaning and spreading my legs for him. Fingers slide through my folds, back and forth, thrusting one in and out of me as they go. His thumb does that delicious thing with my clit intensifying my building orgasm. Two fingers enter me and I'm sure he can feel my walls grasp down on them, needing more. He lets go of my hands and turns me around as his mouth devours mine. My hands grab hold of his hair as he lifts me, wrapping my legs around his wet body and pushes me down on his cock in one thrust filling me, giving me what I need. He's got me up against the wall and I'm riding him, meeting him thrust for thrust, grinding my clit against him.

"You feel so good, Elizabeth. So fucking good."

And he's lifting me and pushing me down on him circling my hips, grinding me against him. And I begin to shatter.

"Marco!"

"Yes, baby....."

"Yes, yes, yes, just like that!"

I feel his cock twitching before he stills and growls, "Fuck, Elizabeth!" He thrusts himself deep and holds me there as my hips jerk against him.

We stand still with only our mouths continuing to devour each other.

He sets me down as he pulls out, we're not able to completely let go yet still spiraling down from our orgasms.

"Love to start everyday like that, Elizabeth."

I have to hold myself up against him because I'm afraid that my legs will give out. "Mmmm, I don't know if I'd ever get anything done."

He laughs softly and brushes his lips softly against mine.

"I'd love to keep you here all day if you can get out of work."

"Oh, I almost forgot. I guess I need to get ready." I almost forgot about work, I'd completely gotten lost in our lovemaking.

"That's too bad," he says with mock hurt on his face. He turns off the water, reaches for a towel and begins to dry me off.

He leaves me in the bathroom to my morning routine. I look at my kiss swollen pink lips and I still feel his delicious mouth on mine while my body is still humming with the memory of his expert hands on me. I expected my reflection to show some sign of what's going on inside of me but it doesn't, not even a hint of all the different emotions swirling around like a whirlpool of water going down a drain.

When I enter the bedroom with the towel wrapped around me Marco's long lean shirtless body is reclined on the bed in only his jeans with the top button undone while his finger is punching into his phone. His legs are crossed at the ankles and he's bare footed. I stop to enjoy this image he gives me, so relaxed and comfortable in my bed it makes me feel giddy and I stop from myself from thinking that's right where he belongs. Hearing me he sets the phone down beside him and casually folds his arms behind his head.

"Dress, Elizabeth. I want to watch you," a sly grin curving his lips.

My jaw drops. His domination is so sexy and think I guess I can play along.

Reaching into my panty drawer I pull out matching black and white lace panties and bra. I don't look at him as I dress, not because I'm shy but I want to imagine him being voyeur and it turns me on. Turning my back to him I bend and step into the panties and slide them slowly up my legs moving my ass as I do.   When I put on the bra my hands brush along my breasts making my nipples harden as I trace a finger along the edges. I slowly take out a pair of thigh high stockings and bend taking my sweet time covering my legs with them. While I decide on what to wear I stand at the door of the closet and give him a good look before I dress in the grey pinstriped slacks, a slate grey sweater and black heels. I put each piece of clothing on methodically knowing he's watching the movements of my body as I do. When I'm done I turn to look at him, his erection is straining against his pants but he hasn't moved an inch. A long moment passes before he says anything.

"You knew exactly what you were doing, didn't

you Elizabeth?" His voice is low and firm sending erotic tremors through me.

I flush and hesitate answering him feeling like I'm going to be punished and heat begins to rise in me.

Quietly I say, "Yes." I'm so turned on by his reaction and I can't believe after all of the sex we've just had between last night and this morning I'm ready to go again.

"You're lucky I'm not going to throw you over my lap and spank that beautiful ass of yours then fuck you hard and fast...this time. Tease me like that again and you can be certain I won't hesitate."

Holy shit! Why do I want to beg him to please do it, the flesh on my ass tingling with just the thought? My pussy is throbbing probably harder than his cock.

"Ok," is all I can manage to croak out between my heavy breaths.

He's commando when we leave my apartment, holding his underwear in one hand nonchalantly with his other arm draped over my shoulder. The clouds are beginning to leave the sky and the ground is covered with wet morning dew from last night's chilly air. Walking down the path to the curb a voice startles me.

"Good morning, Elizabeth," the tone is flat. I turn and see my landlord in front of his portion of the house. There is a beautiful magnolia tree in the front yard that blooms the prettiest white flowers in the spring along with an oak. The magnolia is a grand southern madam that is strong and robust yet delicate and demure. Her leaves are thick, smooth and shiny deep green on one side with a hint of red on the bottom. The hardiness of the tree and leaves shows in the smooth flower petals she graces us with. Mr. Jones is raking up the debris from the trees as they get ready to hibernate for the winter and from the branches that have broken off from the strong winds we've had recently. He's an older gentleman who usually always tries to appear refined which makes me believe he's got a lot of skeletons in his closet. There is something about his demeanor towards me this morning that is unsettling.

"Good morning, Mr. Jones." I try to be friendly even with the strange feeling I'm getting from him. He's always been very personable and open before which is why his attitude today strikes me as strange. He's watching us intently with a serious expression on his face.

Marco senses it as well so he approaches him extending his hand to introduce himself, "Good morning, Mr. Jones, it's a pleasure to meet you. I'm Marco Kastanopoulis."

"Pleasure." He shakes Marcos hand but Mr. Jones' attitude is bordering rude. He doesn't say anything else to Marco to even attempt at being polite so Marco leaves him standing there in his pile of drying up leaves and twigs holding the rake in his hand.

"Enjoy your day, Mr. Jones." I say. He doesn't

reply but just keeps looking at us. I want to get out of this somehow uncomfortable situation fast so I continue towards my Nissan Altima with Marco following me.

"That was...awkward. I've never seen him like that before," I'm confused and I say this more to myself than Marco.

"Is he a nosy old man or just rude?" Marco asks cocking an eyebrow.

"Neither of those usually. But then I haven't had a man here...," and almost say since Santino but I stop myself. There's been enough weirdness for one morning already. I catch the inquisitive look in his eyes wanting to know what I was going to say but he doesn't push me.

Marco closes me in his arms and my hands hold his waist as his lips lightly touch mine. I don't care that I know Mr. Jones is watching us, I shouldn't feel like I have to hide in front of my own home, it's not like we're doing anything inappropriate. I have to fight the urge to turn around to face him and stick my tongue out at him, seems like the perfect thing to do.

"Have a great day, baby. Call you later?"

"You too, Mr. Bond. Talk to you then." And he smiles deliciously at me. I forget all about weird Mr. Jones and his beady little eyes.

About 11:00 Carol walks in to my office and plops down in the chair in front of me. I've got to admit I appreciate the fact this is a busy office and we never get an opportunity to be bored although we all complain about working our asses off. This is probably why none of us feel guilty for stopping for a minute and taking a break to catch our breath.

"You're killing me. How was last night?" Carol looks exasperated.

I giggle, "Or do you mean how was this morning?"

She sits on the edge of her seat, eyes bulging. "He stayed over?"

"Yeah, he wanted to watch me dress...," which was so hot, a crimson blush spreads over my face and chest as I remember it. I decide not to tell her about dessert, some things are just for me.

"That is so hot!" My words exactly, Miss Thing.

"Yes, it was." I feel the heat instantly spread all over my body and I don't think it's from embarrassment and we giggle like two school girls.

"So, when are you seeing him again? It seems like he's got it bad for you, Elizabeth."

That nagging little voice in the back of my head gets a little louder and I just tell her to shut up and go crawl back in to her hole. The common sense side tries to reason with me telling me, 'You're going to have to listen to her sooner or later.' Why does she have to be so damn right all the time?

I sigh, "I don't know, we're not 'seeing each other' seeing each other, it's just sex I guess."

"Common Elizabeth, nobody would go through all the trouble of getting your number like that if they didn't want to see you, like in a formal sense. You're lying to yourself if you think that." Why does she have to be so logical as well, I can't argue with that.

"I know, and you're probably right, but I can't do that, be that with him, or anyone else. At least not right now." Reality check is starting to close in on me and I push it back again, this time having to do it with both hands. Please just let me have a little more time to be happy, just a little more.

"Well, just know what's happening between you two and be honest with yourself...and him, you both deserve it." She stands to leave and smiles warmly at me. She's a good friend, the kind that gently tells you the truth even though you don't want to hear it.

"You're right, Carol. If we keep seeing each other I need to figure this out," I say and smile back at her in a way that says thank you letting her know that I appreciate her honesty even though I didn't ask for it but it's exactly what I need.

I get a text from Janie about 2:00.

Yoga tonight?

Sure, meet you there at 7:00

I haven't spoken to here since we went out and she has no idea about Marco. I know she is going to shit!

The rest of the day goes by and I can hardly remember anything because I'm still on my Marco high. But it's more than that. I feel alive, I feel satisfied and content and I feel like a woman again. What was I just a few short days ago, just a walking meat suit? I feel sexy, feminine and confident. It's crazy but I feel like me again. Where was I? It seems like all of the windows and doors have opened to life and I can breathe again. When I'm with Marco it seems as if time stands still and I just want to live in those moments forever in that tiny moment of eternity when nothing else exists, just us.

At 5:30 I'm at home going through my mail and Marco calls. I think to myself that I've got to get a picture of him for his caller ID and so I can look at him all the time.

"Hi." I feel like a teenager getting a call from her crush.

"Hi. What are you doing?" His voice is low and sexy.

"I'm sitting on the couch going through my mail, feet up on the coffee table. What about you?" Why do I instantly feel aroused?

"Sitting back in my chair at work wishing I had some cookies and cream ice cream and wanting to take a shower. I couldn't stop thinking about you all day, all week really. I think of your scent and it makes me crazy." That's why.

I feel my sex instantly pulse and the wetness begin to ooze, my thighs clench trying to satisfy the growing need between my legs.

"Oh?" is all I can manage, my voice a little high pitched so I clear my throat trying to fix it.

He laughs quietly. "What are you doing tonight? I hope you're thinking about me." Thinking about you, your taste, your touch, your smell.

"Well, yes I am. But I'm meeting Janie for yoga at 7:00. She's one of the girls I was with at the bar the other night, the blonde."

"Oh. I must say I am disappointed. I was hoping I could see you." And I can hear the disappointment that I'm feeling in his voice.

"I'm sorry."

"It's ok. Can I come watch?"

My eyes fly open and I gasp, "No!"

He laughs out loud. "Ok, ok, can't blame a guy for trying. But tomorrow night I have tickets for Thalian Hall. It's our anniversary." I can sense the smile in his voice.

I can barely contain the bubble of excitement rising in me. "That would be really nice, I'd love to go."

"Excellent, I'll pick you up at 6:00, we'll have dinner first. And Elizabeth?"

"Yes?"

"I want you to wear something a bit on the

shorter side for me." His tone changes slightly, dropping, becoming more authoritative.

Throb. Ooze. Ache.

"And one more thing...no touching yourself. Ok?"

I think I'm panting now.

"Ok."

"Good. And do you think you could send me a video of you doing yoga?"

"No!" That manages to get me out of the fantasy I was just starting in my mind.

He's laughing so hard, I can see his face in my head, his eyes crinkling and head back. "I had to try."

"You are so bad."

"Yeah, and you love it."

"Maybe." I'm laughing with him.

"Wait until tomorrow then."

I can hear the promise in his voice of things that I had only longed for, never thinking they could be real, never letting myself hope I would experience. The waiting is going to kill me I'm about ready to cum now just thinking about it. But it's more than my body reacting to it, my heart and soul are too, glowing and bursting with all of the emotions - joy, anticipation, desire, wonder.

"With bated breath." He has me on a rollercoaster ride and I soar with it.

"I love that hot breath, along with the all those little sounds you make, how delicious you taste, and all the hidden little curves of your body. See you tomorrow at 6:00, baby."

He has completely seduced me in two minutes. "I'll be looking forward to it," it comes out as a squeak.

"Not as much as me. Bye." There is a definitely a smile in his voice.

"Bye, Marco."

I sit back on the couch completely turned on and my blood is rushing thinking of his touch. The frustration from the thought of not being able to masturbate to release this ache he's given me is mixed with euphoria at the same time. I'm sure he's done it on purpose knowing this is exactly how I would feel. I'm never going to make it until tomorrow night.

Chapter 5

I walk into the yoga studio at 6:50 seeing Janie's already there laying down her mat so I move towards her and put mine down next to hers. The room is full with a wide variety of people, mostly women but a couple of men as well, since yoga is not considered only for hippies and gurus anymore. The young professionals are easy to spot since they're clad in designer everything from head to toe with perfect artificial nails, tan, and sometimes breasts. The spiritualists are just as easy to identify because they look like they're already tripping on the yoga high. If you've never gotten high from yoga you are seriously missing out on something wonderful. To me, it's the feeling you get when your orgasm is building, it's sensual, warm, and titillating and it carries you away. If that doesn't get you addicted, nothing will.

"Hey you! How's your week?" I greet her feeling I must look like the cat that ate the canary and it was good, its feathers are probably still sticking out of the sides of my mouth.

"Hey! It's good, getting ready for a marathon that's going to include the soccer players from UNCW as some friendly competition. I LOVE soccer players. I can't friggin' wait!"

I laugh at her as she's practically salivating at the idea of all those hot guys sweating alongside of her. She does appreciate a fine looking man.

"You got anything planned for the weekend, Elizabeth?"

Time to come clean. I can't keep the smile from sneaking up on my face as I anticipate her reaction...this is going to be priceless.

"You remember that hot guy from the bar the other night?"

"The one that looked like he wanted to fuck your brains out right there on the bar? The hottie?"

I'm smiling remembering her accurate description of him that night. "Yes, him."

Both of her eyebrows shoot up. "What about him?"

"I'm going to Thalian Hall with him tomorrow."

"You're kidding me?!" The look of surprise on her face is absolutely worth the wait to tell her.

"Nope, he followed me out of the bar the other night."

"What?! And you didn't tell me!" She's almost screeching.

From the front of the room, the instructor greets

the class in her airy salutation with melodic chants floating in the air in the background.

"Namaste'."

And we all repeat, "Namaste'."

I turn to whisper to Janie, "Oh, and he asked if you could video tape me doing yoga so I can send it to him."

"Holy shit!" She hasn't even gotten on her matt yet.

"And no, you're not!" I whisper a shout back at her.

"You are so telling me *everything* when we get out of here!" She whisper shouts back at me.

The instructor is looking right at us along with everyone else in the room. Janie's glare at me says, 'I'm going to kill you for not telling me!' and I can't help but chuckle at her.

"Let's begin with the sun salutation."

Janie gave me a ride back to my apartment after class and we're sitting Indian style on the couch with two bowls of new cookies and cream ice cream on our laps. I've told her how I almost fell on the sidewalk and he came up behind me and caught me, all the way through the events this morning. I leave out the more graphic details though, wanting to keep them tucked secretly away in my little private memories box.

"And you don't want to know what he does with this," I finish, holding out the bowl.

"Ew, I'm eating sex ice cream?!" She scrunches up her face.

"No, this is a new one." I laugh at her as the blush creeps over my skin.

"Then yes I do."

"Sorry, not going there," I tease wiggling my eyebrows at her.

"You suck!" she pouts like a little kid as if someone took her favorite toy and that makes me laugh harder.

After we've scraped all that we can from the bowls we take them back to the kitchen and rinse them out in the sink. Leaning back against the counter she starts to ask me more questions wanting to know the inside details.

"So you're seeing him?"

"I wouldn't say that exactly. We've been having sex. I don't know anything about him and he doesn't know anything about me. No attachments, no trails."

"Hhhmm, I get it." Oh, brother, she's doing that thing with her eyes at me saying, 'I know what you're not telling me'.

"You know, Elizabeth, you won't tell me what you're afraid of that makes you keep hiding."

My brow furrows knowing I have to go there but dreading the answers she might give me. "Have you heard from Santino, Janie? Are you still friends with him on Facebook?"

We've never discussed the details of him leaving and I am so grateful to her for not pushing me to tell her and honestly I'm amazed at her patience. For two years of my life she was right by my side listening to me go on about how much I loved him and how I knew he was the one. Santino and I didn't tell her when he was landing here and we met her for lunch to surprise and to thank her for helping me with the immigration paperwork. She was there for the wedding then two and a half months later he was gone. I stayed away from her for a year after that, pretty much everyone unless I had to associate with them. It was just after that first year he was gone that I started on the Safe Haven project and met Elsie. I guess Janie knew me well enough and figured I would tell her when I was ready. Maybe I'm almost ready.

"I haven't heard from him but I don't know about Facebook, I don't see his name but there are some people I haven't met in person."

She looks at me with caring and concern. She probably thinks I'm missing him and that I've been holding out for him to come back. Yeah, I have but not in the way she thinks.

"Ok."

"If there is some shit, Elizabeth, you need to get it straightened out so you can move on. It's been too long and you're obviously not the only one that's gonna get slammed when it finally hits the fan."

She doesn't know how right she is. And this gives me a cold slap of my reality reminding me that I need to back off of Marco no matter how much I want to dive deep head first into him. I'm walking around in the shadows along the edges with Santino hiding with Marco now, avoiding the fact that I have to move in one direction if I want to get what I want. I know there are mine fields if I go a certain way, ignoring the fact that they'll go off sooner or later.

Friday night 6:00. I stand back and look at myself in the mirror and give the reflection a final review. I chose a demurely sexy short satin backless dress with long sleeves that hug my hips. My hair is up in a French twist giving the back full effect. The dress hints at falling off my shoulders at any moment promising to expose my naked breasts. I fantasize about Marco pushing me up against a wall letting the dress slip down as he pulls my swollen pink nipples between his lips and teeth. He hasn't even gotten here and I am so turned on already I'm aching.

The doorbell rings and I slide on my Jimmy Choo's. My heels click on the hardwood floors matching the pounding of my heart as I walk to the door. I open it and I'm speechless. He's stunning in his casual tuxedo standing there with one hand tucked in his pocket and his head cocked to one side. No man should look this good. Slowly he lowers his look to my feet and scans up my body, to my lips and stops at my eyes. His lips lift seductively up on one side.

"May I come in?"

I blush realizing I was gawking at his delicious appearance. "Oh, yes, please, excuse me."

"No problem. I just didn't want the old man next door having a heart attack watching me say hello to you the way I want to."

If he was any sexier I would be a blubbering idiot. There's and instant inferno inside me as I step aside to let him in. The door closes behind me and he turns to face me.

"Turn around."

My heart rate spikes instantly as I turn. He leans into me as his heavy breathing is by my ear mixing with the sound of my pounding heart.

"Put your hands on the door." His voice whispers low and commanding.

His fingertips are caressing my shoulder and his hot breath is on the back of my neck. Resting my forehead against the door I'm silently pleading for him to run his lips all over me.

"Do you know how badly I want to fuck you right now against this door? Pull that beautiful ass of yours against me and bury myself deep inside you."

My ass involuntarily pushes back onto him begging him to do it. His hardness is against me as his fingers slide down my spine and his teeth press lightly into my neck leaving a mark for everyone to see and I love the thought of it.

Sliding his hands forward inside my dress to my stomach I press harder into him as my body goes rigid. One of his hands travels to my breasts, his thumb on one nipple a finger on the other and he's playing with both. The other hand dips below my panties possessively cupping my sex, sliding his middle finger inside of me as the heel of his palm rubs my clit. He begins to fuck me with his hand and I push down on him, fucking him back. Our bodies are pressed tightly against each other, his pushing me towards the door, mine into him.

"So wet already, baby. Miss me?"

"Yes, Marco." I can hardly get the words out.

My walls begin to clench on his fingers working me towards cumming when he stops.

"Don't stop, please," I moan arching my back.

"You don't know how hard it is. But I have other plans for you tonight, love."

He pulls me against him as he straightens himself. Turning me to face him and staring into my eyes he licks my juices off his fingers.

"I love how you taste, Elizabeth." He pulls me in and claims my mouth.

"Let's go, baby," his voice is deep and gravelly and his eyes are full of desire.

Tonight Marco has a black Lincoln Towncar

waiting for us, the kind used by car services for professional accounts that require formal transportation when a limo is too much. I look at him with a curious expression.

"I thought it would be more convenient to have a driver so we don't have to walk all across town."

"That's very thoughtful, thank you."

He holds the rear door open waiting for me to get in and as I do I glance at one of Mr. Jones' windows. I could swear that I see the curtain falling just as I look. That's very strange. Marco follows me into the car not seeing what I saw. I decide not to say anything thinking I might just be imagining things.

"Good evening, Miss Elizabeth. Ready for dinner, Marco?"

"Yes, please, Joe. Thank you."

"Good evening, Joe," I greet the driver and I see he's wearing a jacket and a tie, impressive. Joe's probably in his sixties and has no southern accent. From what I can tell from his face he looks like a happy go lucky kind of guy with a hint of seriousness about him and I like him instantly.

He pulls up to Circa 1922, just a few doors in from the corner of Front St. and Market St., the minimalistic elegant façade glowing from the soft interior lights. The décor is low key Southern elegance with pops of modernism exhibited in the original artwork hanging on the brick walls. I don't know why but I get a sense of the New Orleans bayou here, maybe because of the antique wrought iron railings used as dividers between the tables along the walls and those at the center of the room.

Marco gets out first holding out his hand to guide me. He whispers close to my ear, "You are the loveliest woman here, Elizabeth, envy of both men and women," and his hand comes to rest on the bare flesh of my back sending electric shocks through me.

I tilt my head towards him and he comes closer. "You are the epitome of beautiful seduction, Mr. Kastanopoulis."

"It's because you bring out the animal in me, Elizabeth." His fingers stroke my skin softly as his nose caresses my ear.

We're standing in front of the maître d' now and our flirting has to come to a halt.

"Good evening, sir, madam, do you have a reservation?" Even though this guy is a bit too full of himself he can't help but put his cocky tail between his legs with Marco in front of him, his presence commands respect.

"Yes, Kastanopoulis."

"Thank you, right this way." Mr. Attitude maître d' turns and leads us through the dimly lit room towards the back of the dining room as Marco keeps his hand possessively on my lower back not breaking the flow of electricity charging between us. I feel beautiful with him, constantly in a state of arousal. Nina Simone's sultry voice is filling the air as she rasps out the words to I Put a Spell on You, Now You're Mine. How appropriate.

The table, again, is intimate and to the side of the room against the wall. I'm beginning to think this is not coincidental. He pulls my chair out waiting for me sit then seats himself next to me. As if by magnetic attraction his hand automatically rests on my upper thigh hidden by the tablecloth with his fingertips just grazing the inside of my leg not moving. By their own will my legs want to instantly part and give him access to move up and stoke the smoldering embers in my groin. He doesn't move and the ache only grows with the need for his touch.

Tonight we have a waiter, a handsome college guy, not as cocky as Mr. Attitude, who probably has a different girl under him every night. He looks respectfully at Marco then his eyes go to my hardened nipples clearly visible through the silky fabric. I don't know if Marco noticed, I'm sure he did, but when he speaks he immediately commands attention.

"Please tell us about your specials tonight," he asks sitting back casually in his chair pulling the waiters attention back to him, power, seduction, and confidence oozing from him. I can clearly see its good being him sometimes. And he knows it. The poor kid has just been dissed. Politely, yes, but dissed none the less. The young man expertly goes through the list not taking his eyes off the image of male perfection sitting next to me. I don't have a coherent idea as to what he's just said, Marco's hand on my thigh has my complete attention.

Marco leans forward crossing his other arm in front of him so his hand is dangling off the table in front of my chest and turns his face to me.

"May I order for both of us tonight, Elizabeth? I believe I know what you like." His fingertips on my inner thigh butterfly upward over my sex.

My breath catches in my throat and my hips squirm under the table as I cross my legs. "Yes, please do." All of my focus has just pinpointed to that spot between my legs where the flame has just been stoked as desire threatens to consume me. Just that slight touch has me spinning.

"The lady will have, (in my head he says 'my cock in that wet hot pussy' and I reply, 'Yes, please, all of it'), the Chicken Orecchiette and I will have the Seared Maine Scallops. Some wine, Elizabeth?" His hand squeezes my thigh.

"Yes...," the single word has so much meaning and he smirks at me.

"And a bottle of the Vigne Del Borgo. Thank you."

"Thank you, sir. I'll bring your wine." The boy is flustered. I'm sure he can sense the sexual tension searing between Marco and I. I wouldn't be surprised if he's getting hard.

Marco hands him the menus with his one hand, the other never leaving my leg. He returns his hand to hang in front of me again and brings his face close to my ear. His fingertip brushes against my nipple and instinctively I move into it.

"Open your legs for me, Elizabeth. Tonight is for experiencing." His face is so close I can feel his warm breath on my skin and my body is screaming to feel his tongue there.

My eyelids dip in desire, a small sigh comes from my slightly parted lips and I do as he asks. He has complete control over me. And I am intoxicated.

"Good. Elizabeth, look at me."

My eyes open and I look deeply into his searing gaze.

"I am your slave, Elizabeth. All I want is to bring you pleasure."

"I'm yours, you have complete control over me, Marco."

"Are you, Elizabeth?" he whispers seductively in my ear as his fingers barely graze over my wetness.

My legs open wider begging for more as his fingertips brush my nipple again. I am in ecstatic agony not being able to react, I'm completely at his mercy. And it's incredible.

"I want more, baby. I want it all." His whisper is a demand.

My breathing is heavy with each lift of my chest touching my rock hard nipple against his perfectly placed finger and its exquisite torture.

The waiter returns with the wine. Marco sits back in his chair as he uncorks the bottle and pours a taste for him. He looks controlled and relaxed and inside I'm a writhing animal in heat.

"I'm sure it's fine, thank you," he says smoothly with his hand still between my legs. In my mind I'm sprawled out on the table and he's fucking me senseless and not one person in the restaurant notices.

The waiter pours two glasses for us and makes a hasty retreat.

We take our glasses, each studying the other, holding them up slightly as in a toast and we drink. I take my hand and place it on his thigh. His hand moves from my leg to my hand and shifts them back to my leg, his hand over mine, and begins to slowly move my fingers up my thigh with his.

"Feel what I feel." Holy shit! He's going to make me touch myself with him, right here in front of everyone.

He pushes our pinkies to brush along my panty line, then feathering the wet lips. My hips react to the erotic touch gyrating slightly.

"Do you like touching yourself with me?"

I can't answer, not with words. My body reacts and he senses it. He sees it with my tongue wetting my lips. He feels it with the fresh escape of wetness seeping from me, and he hears it in my heavy breathing.

"Do you want to make me cum now, Marco?" my words come out in a pant.

"No, baby, I want to make you want to cum all night until it's time." He is sinfully wicked and I'm a puppet in his masterful hands.

He lifts my hand from my lap, brings it to his lips and kisses it then places it back on the table. With one long arm snaking behind my chair he places his hand on my back, sliding it inside my dress until his fingers are caressing under my breast.

"You look radiant, Elizabeth."

"Thank you, Marco." I cannot move. I'm frozen with the onslaught of sensations I'm experiencing. "You were right, Marco."

"Right about what, baby?" Leaning his face into my neck, his breath is a warm ghost of a caress on my cool flesh.

"That tonight is for experiencing." My voice is low and husky.

Bringing his face to mine he kisses me lightly on the lips. He is making love to me completely right here in the most deliciously delicate way and I am melting into his seduction.

"The night is still young, love." And his lips perk up sadistically. The seductive Peggy Lee's Fever is embracing us, What a Lovely Way to Burn.

Our meal arrives and we share our food like long time lovers.

Back in the car Marco pulls me to him so I'm leaning in the crook of his arm while the backs of his fingers stroke my neck. Joe has classical music playing softly, low enough so we can speak comfortably but high enough giving us a sense of privacy.

"We're going to listen to some Puccini at Thalian Hall. I hope you like it."

"I love classical music although I can't identify any of the pieces."

"It's strong and romantic. I think you'll enjoy yourself."

Why do I know there's more to that statement than just the performance?

The theater is small and beautifully intimate. They've kept the feel of the original décor with the deep red curtains, gold burnishing's throughout and crushed red velvet seats. It's breathtaking. Marco's reserved box seats for us and we are alone there. The lights dim and the orchestra and performers are introduced as we take our seats in the darkness.

Marco leans into me and whispers in my ear, "Take off your panties."

My eyes shoot open and my mouth forms a silent O. After a pause I slide the thong down my legs and over my feet without turning my face towards him. He holds out his hand and I look at it. He wants me to give the soaking wet thing to him. I place them in his outstretched hand and he holds them to his face smiling sadistically...then he breathes in deeply and pockets them in his jacket. He puts his arm around my back making little circles with his thumb against my bare flesh and turns his face forward as the music begins. I'm still staring at him completely in shock. And his wicked smile gets even bigger.

It's absolutely beautiful. The music is a journey from soft, to melancholic, to intense and reverberating, I feel it in depths of my soul. The tenor and soprano are superb only adding life to the music.

I have no idea when Marco's hand slid inside my dress from my back. His strokes are the music in movement. They caress my skin softly then build in intensity as the score surges. The sensation as he pinches my nipple when the music crashes makes me throw my head back and gasp loudly. It's the most complete seduction I have ever experienced.

The music lows to deep and intense. Marco's hand is now on my knee and my heart is racing. He kneads my flesh deeply then strokes it softly moving up my thigh. The tempo builds. I spread my legs wide and arch my back. The strings join in with a surging force. Gentle strokes across my wet labia lips. The tenor begins to sing passionately with a deep sadness. A finger is circling my clit enticing my hips to sway with it. The soprano sings to her lover matching his intensity. A finger is stroking inside of me. Meeting the stroking movements that are taking me higher, gripping the sides of the chair fiercely, he's fucking me and I fuck him back lost in the music. The winds join in and the music explodes. He grasps my clit between his fingers and rubs it between them and I cum throwing my head back and clenching my teeth holding the scream in that is bursting from my lungs. The audience stands erupting into applause and Marco and I look at each other, our faces masked with passion. His fingers are still on my clit rocking my body with its pulsing orgasm. Cupping my soaking wet sex in his palm, he brings me back down to earth gently. He takes his hand from me and licks his fingers, my body entirely flushed with desire.

We stand and he straightens my dress. I'm still vibrating from the overload of sensations.

"Common Elizabeth. I need to be inside you. Now."

In the car Marco caresses me lightly stroking my bare flesh and brushing his fingertips against my taut nipples. His arousal is obvious with the huge bulge in his pants and I can't wait to have what's under it buried deep inside of me.

"Did you enjoy the show?" he asks quietly holding me close.

"I believe that was the best show I've ever experienced, thank you." The desire in my voice is evident.

He puts his hand under my chin and turns my face to him, "The pleasure was all mine," his voice gravelly, full of need. His mouth comes down possessively on mine. His lust looks for fulfillment with his tongue stroking mine, licking it and devouring my mouth.

Joe pulls up in front of my apartment. Marco looks deep into my eyes waiting for an invitation. Does he tell the driver to leave?

"Please come in, Marco," I almost pant with the anticipation of what will happen behind my closed door as memories of the breakfast bar send ripples through me.

Turning to the driver and opening the door he says, "Good night, Joe. Thanks for everything tonight. I'll call you again soon."

"Of course, Marco. Have a pleasant evening."

"Good night, Joe. And thank you," I say trying to control my emotions.

"You too, Miss Elizabeth, and you're most welcome."

Marco gets out and holds his hand for me pulling me from the car. I can see in his eyes he can't wait any longer.

Once inside he pushes me against the door, one foot spreads my legs and his hands are on my shoulders pushing my dress down. It stops at my wrists and waist exposing my heavy bare breasts as they point to him wanting to be in his mouth. His lips latch on to one as he pulls his jacket off and throws it to the floor. Sucking and biting one nipple, one hand goes to the other breast squeezing the swollen flesh and pinching the nipple, as his other lifts my skirt and thrusts a finger inside my soaking wet hole. My dress is acting as a bind pinning my arms down, preventing me from touching him. I push myself into his mouth and hands. I can't get enough of him. He's so primal in his need and it makes me wild.

"Fuck, Elizabeth, I've got to have you. Right. Now!" he growls.

"Stop, Marco."

And he abruptly lifts himself from me staring into my eyes with an animal hunger. My hands lift to unbutton his shirt and I begin to walk him back into the apartment. The front of his shirt is open. Lifting his arm I undo the cuff as his bottom hits the chair. I take the other arm and do the same while pushing his feet apart with one foot. He leans back as our eyes watch each other intently. My lips part slightly and his jaw clenches. Reaching down I scrape my nails from his balls all the way up his erection. He throws his head back as another deep growl comes from within him.

"This is mine and I'm going to take it...now."

His head shoots back to face me fixing his eyes on mine wide with anticipation.

I push his shirt roughly from his body scratching his skin lightly with my nails as they trail down to the button of his pants. I don't tease, I'm here to take what I want. What he needs me to take. I drop to my knees with my heels and dress still on and pull off his shoes and socks throwing them aside. I raise my hands and grab both his slacks and boxers and yank them down releasing his raging hard-on and add them to the pile of clothes. Taking hold of his cock with both hands I shove it all the way to the back of my hot mouth swallowing down on it, grabbing the head with my throat.

"Grrrrrrr!" he moans loudly and pushes deeper into me.

I begin to fuck his rock hard cock fast with my mouth, sucking it, licking it, swirling my tongue around the head. I reach one hand down and squeeze his balls cupping them and moving them in my hands then lightly run my nails across the wrinkled skin, My other hand is stroking his shaft, round and round, up and down. Pulling my mouth off to flick my tongue in his hole, I run my hand over the head. He's oozing and I can feel his balls tighten in my hands as his shaft twitches. He puts his hands on the sides of my head guiding my hot mouth down on him. I suck in hard and wrap my tongue around the underside, pulling him all the way in again, clamping down on him in the back of my greedy mouth.

"I'm going to cum, baby!"

And I move faster urging him on. He's guiding me up and down his shaft, his hips thrusting as I hold his throbbing cock firm with both hands stroking him as my mouth sucks, licks and swallows him.

"Aaaahhhhhhh!!" The scream escapes him as I feel the hot cum spirting in my mouth. He holds me still and tenses buried deep in my mouth as I lavish his cock with licks as he cums for me. I feel ecstatic pleasing him like this.

"Fuck, Elizabeth. I need more of you!" Pulling

me up he shoves his tongue in my mouth fiercely and I suck on it needing to fill myself with him somehow.

He wraps me in his arms and carries me to the bed with his still hard erection against me. Setting my feet down and pulling off my dress he throws it to the floor then takes a handful of my breasts, kneading them and devouring my mouth while my nipples are between his fingers, pulling and flicking them.

"Take your hair down. I want to feel it on my skin, baby." I love it when he commands me with that husky sexy voice of his.

I pull out the pins and drop them to the floor, swinging my hair free. Marco takes a hand full and rubs his face in it, breathing deeply.

"Sooooo good...,"

Pushing me back on the bed with my legs hanging off the edge he pulls me down so my ass is at the edge. Shoving my legs open and holding them wide he kneels down and buries his face there, savagely lapping up my juices. Now it's his turn to take what he wants.

"Yes, Marco!" My fingernails are digging in to the bed and I know if it was his skin I would draw blood.

We are not going to make love, we're going to fuck like animals in heat, primal and primitive. Our need blinding us where all we can see and feel is lust.

His tongue is fucking me with such ferocity, circling and sucking my clit. I'm riding his face needing more, pulling it hard against my pussy. Pushing me up the bed, he's on top of me rubbing himself along my wet folds, stopping to tease my clit with it. I wrap myself around him, my throbbing clit screaming for friction, my pussy grabbing emptiness searching for his cock.

"Please, Marco, I want you inside me."

"Fuck, Elizabeth!" and he plunges all the way in filling me instantly.

"Yes, Marco, more, hard..."

He begins to thrust in and out, my legs wrapped around his waist, slow, hard and deep. Grinding against me, circling my hips on him, I push back against him.

His tongue is mimicking his thrusts in my mouth as his fingers are teasing my nipple, pinching and twisting it. He's thrusting hard and deep as my nails scratch up his back, pulling a deep moan from him. Our bodies separate as we fuck and we both look down to watch him moving in and out of me. I grind into him watching our pelvises dance and rock together. The sight of our hips slamming into each other is so sexy and so erotic it intensifies our movements heightening our passion. He can feel my walls clenching him, grasping his cock and he flips me over rough and demanding. Lying on my stomach he spreads my legs and lowers his body to mine as my ass rises slightly to meet him. He pounds deeply into me pushing against my cervix.

His hand comes down my stomach to my clit possessing it and I begin that leap over the edge. He thrusts and flicks and it feels so good. I feel it building and spread my legs wider wanting him deeper. Lifting us both, pulling my ass in the air, he gives me just what I need. He runs his hand through my juices around his cock sliding in and out of me with a wet finger now making circles around my other hole.

"I want this too, Elizabeth. I want all of you." The sound of his voice is full of hot need.

"Oh, God, Marco," I moan into the bed.

His thrusts deepen and become faster.

"Yes, yes, yes, Marco!" I slam back on him fucking him hard, exploding, pulling the orgasm from him at the same time.

"Oh, God, Elizabeth!" Buried in to his balls, he grinds into me as his fingers tighten on my clit. It's so much, too much stimulation and I can't control the force of my orgasm, everything is pulsing and throbbing, grasping and sucking as I shatter, my body vibrating in its tremors.

"Yes, yes, yes!!!!!"

I rub myself onto his fingers and his throbbing cock inside of me riding the wave of sensations. It's glorious, our bodies taking from the other, sucking the other dry to satisfy our hunger.

We collapse on the bed, still joined by our throbbing sexes.

"Jesus, Elizabeth...," he's panting hard against my neck.

"Wow...," I breathe out heavily.

"You're like a drug, Elizabeth, and I can't get enough of you, I want more." Our bodies are rubbing against each other, he's holding me tight stroking his face against me, as we move together still in the throes of our lingering passion.

I don't know what to say. The words 'take it all' are on my lips begging to come out but I can't say them. The storm I know will come has invaded our intimacy bringing its dark clouds with it. It's time for me to stop putting things off and do what I should have done a long time ago. Before it's too late.

I turn in his arms and pull him close to me, my lips softly touching his.

"Thank you for tonight. Everything was amazing."

"Anything for you, baby. You were so intoxicating at the show, Elizabeth. I was completely captivated watching your face."

"Marco, what you made me experience tonight was truly unbelievable. I was soaring through the stars, a high I've never experienced before. It was absolutely amazing." My smile is so big I feel I'm going to burst.

He nuzzles his face in my hair holding me tighter.

"I am so glad. I told you, all I want to do is bring you pleasure, the most you've ever had. And it's only the beginning, Elizabeth, there's so much more to come."

"You have, by far, gone beyond that." The joy I'm feeling is overflowing as I cover him in tiny bites and kisses. But those storm clouds are pulling me back, keeping me from basking completely in this afterglow. I try very carefully to keep everything in the now with Marco, staying in the moment. I don't make any references to tomorrow or any promises, I don't let myself expect any and I don't give any. This moment right now is all that matters. Promises or tomorrow will only ruin it.

He leans back laughing at me, searching my face.

"Do you have plans tomorrow?"

"No..."

"Do you just want to hang out with me?"

That sounds funny coming from him but perfect as well.

"Absolutey." Please, just a little more time of happiness. Please, I silently beg.

Chapter 6

I'm standing in a very large room filled with people dressed in medieval clothing and there's a huge fireplace, big enough for 4 men to stand erect in, with a blazing fire burning. It's a royal court and I'm me but not in this body. Everyone is elegantly dressed and as my focus turns I see at the far end a raised platform with two large chairs, I presume they are the thrones and in one sits a strikingly handsome dark haired man with a crown resting elegantly on top of his head. He is the king and seated on the floor in front of him is a beautiful young blonde woman, the king's footholder. He looks down to her with affection in his eyes and his mouth moves as he's saying something to her. It's strange but I don't hear any voices but I know what's being said in my head, even with the different voices around me I can sense the buzzing of words. The footholder turns and looks at me and there's fear in her eyes. He wants her in his bed but she's afraid of me. Good, he's my husband. But I know it's only a matter of time before she ends up in it, just like her, and I turn to find the ravishing redhead that I know has shared my husband's bed since I conceived our first child. My eyes rest on the striking woman, fire from the top of her head to her feet with gold dripping from around her neck, wrists, fingers and from her ears, the rewards for jobs well done. Her red dress only adds to her fire and I can feel my hate for her flowing through my body. Her green eyes look pityingly at the footholder knowing that the amateur is no match to her womanly skills. My husband the king looks fondly towards me and raises his hand calling me to him and I must oblige, he wants to be surrounded by all his whores. I know he loves me and I am above all of his other women, I'm the queen and I have the crown to prove it, but the snide looks and quietly whispered insults behind my back as I walk by still hurt none the less. After three children I am still beautiful and my body has evolved into a voluptuous beauty, evident in my purple gown as my white cream breasts move, wanting to spill out of their confinement. I take my seat next to my king looking at him and I can't help but still feel the love I have for him. I am to his right and to his left stand his knights, all except one, my lover. He's asked for someone to fetch him as the king wants his whole court with him.

I love him too, passionately, wildly, as a woman not a queen. And he takes me as a woman, hard and rough with a burning fire, and then other times he adores and worships me calling me his only queen. I came to him first not being able to resist him, the hunger pulled me to him and he tried to resist, tried to stay loyal to his king but he loved me as well. I find him in the stairs going to our tower and he pushes me down lifting my skirts and takes me like an animal from behind on the cold hard stones and I cry out in my passion for him never getting enough because he holds a part of himself from me and it breaks my heart. The last image I have is of me standing alone in the early morning twilight on a muddy road looking out in the distance waiting for my knight who I know will never return.

I have had this dream many times and I know now that Marco is my king, he always has been I just had never known the man until now but I've always known that my lover, my knight, my warrior was Santino. We have all lived before, together in another time.

"Mmmmmm," sleep begins to lift from me replaced with need as the sun caresses our skin with the lingering feelings of my dream still warming me. Marco's fingers are teasing me and tantalizing me awake. One nipple is being plucked by his lips and two fingers inside me have worked me into a heated frenzy. My back to his front, his hard-on wedged between my dampened thighs as he's sliding it through my clenched thighs. I reach down and stroke the head wet with his pre-cum and my desire as his cock jumps at my touch. Feeling my orgasm wanting release, I guide him inside me while his hand pushes down on my mound bringing us closer together. His thrusts hit that magic spot and I still as my walls clench tightening around him. His rhythm is slow, pulling out then pushing in deep. Putting my hand over his, he slides both of our hands to my clit, taking my finger with his, circling it, teasing it back and forth. Lowering our hands, fingers scissored, I slide his cock between them feeling it moving in and out of me. The small gesture is so erotic and intimate I feel both of us react to it.

"Oh, God, baby," he murmurs deeply against my back as I feel the vibrations of his voice echo inside of me.

I'm about to fall head first down that orgasmic precipice. Pushing both of the heels of our palms down on my clit, I tumble and it's glorious. I feel his cock harden as he thrusts deeper, stilling, burying himself, pressing me hard against him. And his long, deep growl vibrates against me.

I love morning sex.

"What would you like for breakfast, baby?" he asks quietly moments later, nuzzling my neck.

"You know, I usually don't eat breakfast but for some reason I'm famished, Marco," I tease him.

He laughs, "I am too. I think we'd better get some nourishment in us, we might need it later for energy."

We're at the breakfast bar, he's sitting down having his coffee in his divine self in those lovely boxers, me leaning into him between his legs holding my tea dressed in a cami and shorts. He's stroking my legs, his smile is so relaxed.

"I'll cook. I did learn a few things at that diner as a kid."

"Really? Even better." Thank God, I am definitely not the greatest cook.

He stands and goes to the fridge as I take his place on the chair. He's a wonderful sight moving around the kitchen looking right at home. His natural confidence is truly a ray of sunshine flowing brightly from him and it warms me making me smile.

"Well, it looks like all we have is breakfast stuff," he turns grinning at me. "What do you eat, Elizabeth? We should go to the store later. If we don't we might starve."

I lower my head laughing in playful embarrassment. "I know, it's so sad. Usually I'll just have a salad of some kind when I get home. You know, just me and all. I don't usually have dinner parties, Mr. Kastanopoulis."

He laughs as I watch him take out the pans, eggs, spinach, pan spray and some spices. There are some whole wheat wraps he finds in the pantry as well.

"You know, I don't know much about you, Elizabeth. You're very private," he asks as he turns the stove on to sauté the spinach.

I turn my face to look away and try not to let my walls close in on me. "Well, there isn't too much to tell."

"You have so many fantastic pictures of your

family. I hope you don't mind I was looking at them." He's fishing for information but he's being very polite about it.

"No, not at all." I smile more to myself thinking back on those moments in the photographs. "Yeah, we were very close..." My mind visits more than just the places but the closeness as well that was lived in those pictures and I turn to look at him. He's whisking the eggs and glances at me waiting to see if I'll continue, giving me some space.

"I am the youngest of five children," I begin. "My parents had an international grocery store in Westchester County in New York where I grew up. Both of my parents are deceased now." It still hurts to say that, more than I ever would have realized.

He's still quiet and I'm not quite sure he's satisfied with just my life blurb, not that there's anything very exciting about my 'so-called life'. So, I continue. He deserves at least that much.

"Like your parents, mine worked themselves almost to death. Neither of them graduated from high school, I don't even know if my mother attended high school, but they were the poster children of the American dream. Work hard and you'll make it. My parents really didn't participate in our lives while we were growing up because they were always working, they were the best, absolutely amazing. To this day my brother's friends talk about how much they loved my mother."

I pause and he's still silent waiting for me continue.

"I didn't really care for school. My brother and sister were popular, I was well known, likeable but not well liked. I don't know if I developed the bitch persona because of that or because I was a bitch was the reason I wasn't well liked. Anyway, I graduated high school early and moved to the city to start my life. A year later I got a job with the designer. Sometime after that, I started to live the city life, you know, probably like you. My parents had retired down here by that time. Then a few years later the company began restructuring and people were being fired on their lunch hour. It was summertime so I decided to leave and take the summer off and do what young people do in New York. My parents kept asking me to come down here and help them with a business they had bought. I, of course, refused so they sent my brother to come and get me. I cried the whole way down. But I realize now it was for the best looking back. And here I am." I raise my hands in finality.

He turns to me with two mouthwatering plates of spinach egg wraps and two bottles of water.

"I'm sorry to hear about your parents. It sounds like you loved them very much."

And it's true, no matter how old you are when both of your parents are gone you can't help but feel like an orphan. There is so much sincerity in his face I can't look at him because of the lump in my throat. He deserves so much more but that's all I can give him right now.

"Thank you. And this smells wonderful, thank you again."

He leans in to kiss me tenderly. "You are welcome."

We eat in silence making those eyes like 'This is so wonderful' moaning in satisfaction.

When we're done and sitting back content, he looks mischievously at me and says, "Well, Elizabeth I think we need a shower," and swoops me up over his shoulder. Peals of laughter echo through the apartment as I'm pretending to protest the whole way to the bathroom, kicking my feet and screaming. Turning the water on with me still over his shoulder he puts us both in, clothes and all, while the water is still cold.

After the shower we sit on the couch relaxing, I'm in a robe, he's in a towel. His head is lying on my lap as I'm playing with his beautiful damp hair.

"I've called Joe to come and get me."

"Ok." My heart drops but I try to keep the hurt from showing on my face. I should have known, shouldn't have gotten caught up in silly ideas of romance and hearts and flowers. It serves me right, though. I wasn't supposed to be doing this in the first place. I've learned that lesson too well already so I guess it's payback time. "Well then, you should get up and get dressed." There's a slight bitterness in my voice even though I try to make light of it.

"I can't go walking around in those clothes all day, baby." He says noticing my tone and I can see the surprise on his face.

I laugh, relief flooding me, but I'm still feeling guarded. I shouldn't just trust, shouldn't just open myself up, kicking the door open and say, 'Common in.' I did that before and it got kicked in, smashed, and left me lying on the ground beaten and I'm still trying to clean up the mess. Besides, I can't open it, no matter if he's banging on that door demanding to be let in or not. What have I gotten us into?

"No, that would look a bit out of place. They have a saying down here, 'Dirty Stay Out'. I think that ensemble would definitely fit that category, regardless of how amazing you look in it." I joke, trying to make it seem like I don't care one way or the other.

"So, I thought I'd go and change and come back and pick you up. Does that sound alright?" He notices that I've withdrawn and he tries to soothe me. Guilt stabs me but my defenses are already up. He doesn't owe me anything, we haven't made any promises to each other and I have none to give. We're just having sex, no more, no less.

"Great. It will give me time to get dressed and get some things done."

"Good," he says smiling. His phone beeps so he takes it out to check it. "He's here, baby," pulling my head down, he places a light kiss on my lips then heads into the bedroom to get dressed.

My head falls back on the couch and I try to calm the mixed emotions swirling inside of me. "Shit, just relax."

He comes out dressed and I walk him to the door as he wraps his arms around me, kissing me deeply. Looking into my eyes he says reassuringly, "I'll see you in about an hour."

"Alright, see you then." And I watch him walk out, holding his jacket over his shoulder as my heart cracks just a little. Why do I feel so vulnerable right now?

An hour later I'm dressed in skinny jeans and a black thermal. My iPod is on the dock and Meg Myers' Desire begins her seduction. I'm lying on the couch as I get lost in the words. My fingers begin to tease my breasts as an ache grows deep in my loins. I scrape a fingernail over the seam on my sex and unbutton my jeans, arching my back. Sliding one hand down my pants, the other up my shirt cupping my breast, my body starts to writhe. What has Marco done to me, I want him inside me now, I'm on fire.

I don't hear the door open while I'm lost in my world. He's on me. His hands slide down mine inside my pants mixing with my finger in my sex while his other is twisting my nipples but I still don't open my eyes.

"Take me now, Marco, please...," I moan.

He pulls my shirt up, pulls down one cup of my bra and greedily pulls the hardened nipple into his mouth, teasing the point with his tongue as his hands are jerking my pants down. Positioned between my legs he begins to slowly slide into me. His teeth bite my lip as his tongue flicks the captive skin. His thrusts are slow and shallow moving his hips up, rubbing my clit as he enters. Biting my jaw and licking my neck, his mouth consumes me, finally coming down on mine and slowly caressing my tongue with his.

The heavy breathing of Lana Del Rey's Burning Desire fills the air with our own. He feels my walls grasping down on him, pulling him in more as he continues his slow shallow thrusts building me higher. My nails score over his ass cheeks, pushing him harder into me, begging him to push me over the edge. He answers my need and buries himself all the way in and holds himself there while pinching my nipples, giving me that extra sensation to tip me over. And I cum slow and languid, floating in bliss.

"Oh, God, oh God, oh God..." I'm spinning, spiraling, doing that cosmic dance.

He begins to thrust into me again deep and fast. I feel his cock throbbing as he buries himself, his face in my hair, growling. I feel his release in me and I grind into him, moaning. His arm wraps tightly around my waist holding me close, as we lie silently together, coming down from our blissful ride.

"Hi, Marco...," I whisper into his ear as I lick it. My desire for this man is insatiable.

"Hi, baby...," he breathes heavily as he sucks on my neck sending aftershocks through me making me shake with them.

"Mmmmmmmmmm."

He sighs heavily, smiling. "I'm gonna get a towel, love, be right back."

I watch his ass as he walks away in only his shirt. He is so sexy I could just watch him all day and soak in him. When he comes back he's grinning and still semi-hard, his erection glistening with our juices. Lifting my legs and sitting down, he places my feet on his thigh, opening and separating my legs, leaving me wide open to him.

"Lift up," he says his eyes fixed on my swollen sex. He puts a towel under my bottom then begins to trace circles around my sex. I'm watching him looking at me, his eyes fixed and hungry. He takes his shirt off. That finger then slides down my folds and circles my entrance. I feel the cum dripping from me and my eyes widen. His eyes rise to mine and he's smiling seductively.

"It's so sexy watching my cum drip from you, Elizabeth." He swirls that finger around my entrance again, tracing it with his cum. That is so hot!

A new wave of desire flows through me as he pushes that finger inside of me beginning to fuck me again with it and I feel tinges of my last orgasm stirring. I watch his cock as it hardens, growing, turning red with the blood that's filling it. He twists his finger, curving it so that he's rubbing that spot inside me. His other hand wraps firmly around his shaft at that base.

"Touch your breasts, baby," he commands huskily.

I pull my top up and release the other breast, pushing the cup down, forcing both of them up. I begin to move my hips as my finger traces circles around my pebbled nipples.

"Keep your hips still, this is mine."

I stop and my sex instantly clasps onto his finger and he smiles at me, feeling my reaction to his command.

"You like it when I talk to you like that, Elizabeth." It's a statement, not a question, one he's certain of. And this makes my sex clench him again.

His look intensifies with my body's response to his commands. He begins to slide in and out again slowly turning his finger around inside of me as he strokes himself. He stops to rub the pre-cum of his beautifully engorged head, making it glisten. I pull on my nipples and squeeze the swollen globes as his thumb flicks across my clit.

I gasp loudly, throwing my head back and push my ass down, clenching down on his finger. He's finger fucking me and fucking himself as I'm teasing and playing with my nipples. My sex is holding on to his finger tightly still swollen from our lovemaking and I feel my climax ready to push me over the edge again. My body belongs to him, it responds to his every command. I'm helpless, and it's wonderful.

"Cum with me, Elizabeth," the words firm and deep.

His thumb pushes down on my clit as his finger curls on that spot inside of me. I grasp onto my nipples tightly, pinching them as the erotic pain shoots to my pussy and I come undone. My hips grind into his hand as my sex spasms on his finger.

"Yes, yes, yes!!" I whisper in ecstasy.

Throwing his head back and lifting his hips to the hand holding his cock, his orgasm explodes all over his stomach as another growl comes from him. He lowers his face to place a sucking kiss on my clit.

"Oh, God, Marco," I moan.

"That was so beautiful, baby," he murmurs adoringly as he strokes both me and himself.

He begins the job of cleaning me first, then him, and he looks like he's thoroughly enjoying himself. When he seems like he's finally satisfied with the results he stands, bends to kiss me and says, "Be right back," and heads back towards the bathroom.

Holy shit! What just happened? I'm stunned momentarily. The music is still playing with 30 Seconds to Mars' Hurricane. Wiping myself first with the towel still tucked under my ass, I get up and begin to dress.

Marco returns. I can't help but admire his naked body again making my breath catch slightly and I hope he doesn't notice. His lips quirk up, he noticed.

"Interesting compilation of songs, love." He pulls me to him smiling down at me.

"It's my 'feel sorry for my horny self' collection." Shrugging, I laugh.

"Feeling sorry for yourself, baby?"

"Not actually, I guess I was horny," blushing deeper, the last tinges of my earlier uncomfortableness slipping away. For guys it's easy for them to be honest and open about their desires and I can't believe that I'm at a place with Marco that I feel I can say these things so freely to him.

"Still horny, Elizabeth?" he whispers seductively in my ear.

"It's a perpetual horniness with you, Marco. You make me burn." My voice is still raspy from the lingering effects of my orgasm and I'm flushed and heated.

"Dragon, baby." His hands are on my ass holding me close as his lips brush my ear with his words.

He releases me and goes to get his clothes to dress. Pulling on his boxers and pants, he asks me, "Want to go to the store now? I have a feeling we're going to be famished soon." He winks at me and I throw a pillow at him, laughing.

He laughs looking at me with a warning in his eyes, "Oh, yeah? You wanna play?"

I squeal and take off running away from him. Making a few laps around the living room, I'm the hunted and he's the hunter, he pounces on me and throws me to the couch kneeling straddling me on my lap he pins me down with my arms to my sides. He hasn't even broken a sweat and I'm panting. Looking into his face I see his expression change becoming stronger like a predator with a hint of intimate satisfaction. My pulse quickens and I don't know if my panting now is from the play or the vibes coming off Marco.

Holding me down his voice is low and sexy, there's something different about it and it sends sensual tremors through me, "Do you submit, Elizabeth?"

Heat seeps through my veins and my mouth opens slightly as my tongue begs for him. "I do," I whisper, my heart slamming against my ribcage. The woman that I've kept locked up who's been waiting to submit wakes from her slumber and is at full attention ready to be tied.

Leaning his face slowly to mine, his tongue teasing my mouth, quietly he says, "Not yet, baby, but you will." His mouth claims mine with all of the promises in that one little answer.

We walk leisurely through the aisles at the grocery store completely relaxed falling in step with each other as if we've done this a hundred times. Marco's pushing the cart and I have my arm hooked over his elbow. We've picked up a French baguette, swiss cheese, fruits, asparagus, endive lettuce mix, a bottle of chardonnay (he picked it out), some baby potatoes, chicken breasts, and various other things. We are in no hurry so we're just looking around at all of the selections. This is one of the high end chain grocery stores so there is a wide variety of high quality items. We come across a children's sunglass display in all sorts of funny designs so I pull out a monkey pair with bananas on the frames and put them on.

"Do you think they're me, Marco?"

He doesn't bat an eye but reaches for his own pair.

"Those are amazing but I think these are better," and he slides on a hot pink pair covered in rhinestones with huge stars on the corners. We're laughing at each other when I hear my name.

"Liz?"

I turn with the glasses still on and I feel like the floor drops out from under me.

"Hi, Adriana, how are you?" My voice is flat and there's shock written all over my face. Marco and I take our glasses off and put them back on the rack. Fuck. I turn slowly to the woman bracing myself.

"I'm good, you know, I don't like to complain. How've you been?" No, she doesn't like to complain but she enjoys making you feel like shit because you haven't been in touch with her and she knows she looks like hell.

"I've been good." I answer short and sweet, let's make this quick.

And her eyes move to Marco, starting at his feet

her eyes scan him taking everything in and move all the way up to his face. Even if she's not well she's still the ever-flirting bitch she always was. She holds her hand out to him, palm down, the way a woman extends her hand to a man when she wants him to kiss the top. My blood is boiling.

"Hi, I'm Adriana, Elizabeth's big sister."

I can see the look of surprise on his face he's trying to conceal with a gracious smile that he's perfected. He takes her extended hand and shakes it but does not kiss it. Good!

"It's a pleasure to meet one of Elizabeth's family. I'm Marco Kastanopoulis." Oh, he's very good.

"The pleasure is all mine." What a cunt, she never changes even after everything.

"I didn't know you shopped here." I drag her attention away from the man I'm with and back to me. I'm not giving Miss Black Widow any opportunities with him.

"I usually don't, it's for a client."

"I see." This is getting excruciating.

"Have you spoken to Ray," and she turns back to Marco, "our brother?"

"Yes, I called him last week," dragging her shark stare back to me.

"And all is well with his family?" I can't stand the 'poor me', fake sugar sweetness.

"Yes, everyone is great." My politeness is rapidly running out.

Then she leans in a little to me, glancing up at Marco, lowering her voice saying, "And Santino?" I can't BELIEVE she just went there!

"Adriana, I told everyone over two years ago that was over. Don't mention it. Ever." My voice is hard and threatening.

"I'm sorry," no, she's not, "I don't want to ruin your day." Here goes the 'poor me' crap again. "Well, I'll let you get on with your shopping. It was good to see you, Elizabeth." Turning to Marco she continues, "It was nice meeting you, take good care of my little sister, Marco," she purrs with a seductive smile. God, she infuriates me.

"It was very nice meeting you, Adriana. Maybe we'll see each other again," he replies smiling politely, then looks at me.

"I certainly hope so," so she can try to fuck you too, the words scream in my head. "Bye, Elizabeth, you look really good."

"Bye, Adriana, thanks."

And she finally walks away. I look at Marco smiling trying to compose myself.

"So, what else do we need?" I try for nonchalant but end up with icy.

He's studying me. "Hmm, let's have a look around." He knows I'm upset so he gives me some space and anchors me by putting his arm around my waist as he continues to lead me down the aisles. I'm stiff with the anxiety of seeing her but it doesn't stop him from holding me as he's trying to ease some of the tension from my body.

We go to check out and, fortunately, there are no more sightings of Adriana.

The ride home is fairly quiet with very little small talk. Finally, Marco just covers my hand with his and lets the music fill the space giving me time to decompress in my own little world. He's changed it to modern rock and Linkin Park belts out Numb which matches my mood perfectly.

When we get to my apartment we begin to unload the groceries from his car. The leaves are all but gone from the trees and Mr. Jones is in his yard raking them again. Doesn't this guy have anything else to do? I really don't know where all of these leaves have come from because the Magnolia and Oak don't lose their leaves. He's staring at us so we nod our greetings to him. Jerking his head, he starts to jab at the innocent leaves and ends up pulling the grass up with them. What the fuck is his problem now? I know that if he says anything at all I'm going to go off on him and tell him what a complete rude ass he is. I have never seen him act so weird. I'm a grown woman and I think his attitude can't possibly be because I have a man with me. And the man I have with me shows he is obviously a respectable and confident gentleman. Marco and I just look at each other and shrug. He noticed it as well.

As we're putting the groceries away Marco decides to address the gigantic elephant in the room.

"It seemed like your sister was very glad to see you. I can see the similarities but I don't know if I would have known you were sisters if she hadn't told me." Boy, he is so diplomatic.

"Good," I snort.

He laughs. "I guess you weren't very happy to see her."

"Hah, whatever gave you that idea?"

"Maybe it was the way she was flirting with me. Or how you hissed at her when she mentioned Santino." There, it's all out, elephant sufficiently addressed, at least this part.

I freeze then slowly turn to Marco trying to control my emotions. It's not his fault and I shouldn't take it out on him so I silently pull in the remains of my anger, first from Adriana then from Mr. Jones. Marco deserves some kind of an explanation and not a knife throwing crazed female.

"This isn't the first time she's flirted with the man I'm with but at least she's progressed to not doing it behind my back anymore. And Santino is the past. She should have left it there." I dismiss it. I can't tell him about Santino, not yet. I can sense the walls of the past slowly beginning to close in on me.

Marco comes to me and holds me in an embrace,

tenderly kissing me on the top of my head.

"Elizabeth, nothing you could tell me could ever change my opinion of you. As I've said before you are a very private person, even making me keep things about myself from you. I don't know what your reasons are but I'm sure to you they're very good ones. My hope is that soon you will trust me enough to let down those walls and let me in. Now, let's put this behind us and enjoy the rest of our day together." Holding me at arm's length, looking me deep in the eyes, he continues, "Ok, baby?"

I smile at him as relief overtakes my frustration. "Ok," the word comes out in an exhale and I put my arms around his waist as the tension I've been holding in slips slowly away from me. He feels it and smiles bringing his lips to mine, kissing them softly, biting them gently, licking and tasting them before sliding his tongue to join with mine. When his mouth leaves me he rests his forehead against mine with satisfaction showing on his face as well. I don't understand why this man has not run away from me yet with the bag full of insinuated secrets I constantly carry around with me. I am so much more trouble than I'm worth.

"Let's have some lunch then why don't we go to the Cape Fear Museum. Have you ever been?"

"No, I haven't, that sounds great. I'll do the lunch."

He laughs out loud saying, "That's 'cause that's the easy meal."

"And I'm not the one with the talents which,

may I say, you have many," and I smile seductively at him.

Marco brings his lips close to mine whispering, "And we're only just beginning, my love," taking my lower lip between his teeth.

I moan, my body falling into his warmth. Thoughts of Adriana and my reality fade to the back of my mind into a distant silent nag as my only focus is this moment forgetting I was in prison and I want nothing more than to be free.

It's late afternoon before we head to the museum. The building is a small facility, its design is androgynous, not modern or historical, just a big square brick building. The displays showcase different aspects of the local past, the area's link to WWII, a Maritime pavilion, currently something on the progression of communication through history, also giving a different perspective on the originations and growth of the area. We hold hands, walking the hallways and standing in front of exhibits as we listen to the robotic animations and read the synopses'. It's not far from my place but a little too far to walk so, again, he drives the Bond-mobile. I see some clients from work and we exchange hellos and smiles. Marco looks to me inquisitively and I smile saying one word in explanation, 'work'. I see a look of disappointment pass his face quickly and guilt stabs me again. It's not fair to him but I rationalize it by saying to myself, 'That's how he started this thing between us, mysterious and non-committed. No introductions, questions, or expectations'. But does it really make me feel better?

Back in the car after we leave I get a text from Janie.

What are you doing tonight?

I'm with Marco.

So, you're doing Marco?

Lol, (I really laugh out loud).

Marco looks over at me smiling. "What's so funny?"

"Janie."

Parking in front of my apartment, I show him the conversation and he laughs too.

"She sounds great." Again, an instant of frustration mars his features accompanied with another stab of guilt in me. Not wanting to ruin the day I push it aside and come back to the moment.

"Yeah, she is. I'm really lucky she calls me a friend."

"She's lucky to have you as a friend, Elizabeth. Anyone would be lucky to have you in their life." Squeezing my hand, he peers deeply into my eyes. What does he mean? What exactly does he want from me? His innuendos and complete attention have me spinning in confusion. What are we doing here? I am as much to blame, knowing full well I can't offer him anything more but not being able to stay away.   He has breathed life into me and I am addicted to him and I'm afraid I can't give him up.

Looking away, I smile. "Thank you."

"Hey, I guess I've got dinner to start. Common."

When we go inside he sits me on the counter, pours us each a glass of wine, touches his lips to mine and begins to prepare the chicken. I watch him quietly admiring him for all that he is.

"You couldn't have learned to cook like that at your parent's restaurant."

He peeks at me sideways with a crooked smile.

"No, I enjoy cooking. There was a point in my life it helped me to relax. I cooked a lot and bought cookbooks and experimented with different things. It was like therapy to me during a stressful time in my life."

I don't say anything. We gaze at each other with understanding and compassion knowing we are both scarred and damaged spirits who have found the other while demanding nothing. Just accepting what is given and giving fully in return. But for how long? It seems like the time is running out on that clock.

Marco's meal is superb. He's done chicken breasts with a cream sauce and rosemary roasted potatoes with endive salad topped with warmed balsamic vinaigrette dressing on the side. I can't believe this sophisticated and sexy man can cook like Julia Childs. Thinking of my cooking abilities, or lack of, I don't know if I'll ever cook for the man.

After dinner we sit on the couch with a glass of wine and a piano concerto playing in the background just enjoying being together. This is what normal people do every day, just another part of their everyday life. They go out, do things together, stay at home and enjoy each other's company and live. I should be able to do normal things and live my life and not just exist, hiding in my warm and safe prison that I've created, afraid of what's going to happen if I do. I've lived like that for so long I stopped hearing the calling of my soul begging to be set free. Marco came along and gave me a glimpse of what being alive feels like again, truly alive, to feel deeply, what it is to feel pleasure without risk of condemnation, but more than anything, to be sincerely appreciated. I can't do it anymore; I can't go back to what I was before.

"Marco, I have to tell you something. You have completely amazed me. I almost have to apologize to you." I feel so content here in this moment with him, so grateful for everything he's done for me that he's completely unaware of.

Cocking a brow surprised by that he asks, "Why?"

"Well, when I first saw you in the bar with that blonde bimbo falling out of her clothes all over you, I thought you were a pretentious playboy snob. That is so far from the truth about you. You are an amazing man. You're kind, sincere, and you are the complete opposite of pretentious. Granted, yes, you are extremely confident and sexy but not in any negative sort of way. But I did see a hint of that alpha male in you come out at Circa,"

He laughs at that remembering that night. "What? He was looking at your tits. It was better that way than knock him on his ass."

I laugh almost shocked. "You wouldn't have."

"Yes, I would have. No one has the right to look at my woman like that."

The off-handed comment leaves me stunned. 'His woman'. How do I feel about that? To be honest, I feel like I've just won the lottery. I want to belong to him, to totally and completely be possessed by him. But I can't do that, not yet.

He continues, "And let me clarify about that blonde bimbo, she works for an associate of mine and wouldn't leave me alone and I didn't want to be rude. If you noticed, never did I lay a finger on her. You were the only woman that I saw." His look at me is penetrating.

"Then why didn't you come and talk to me?"

"I never got the opportunity. The men were hounding you. Besides, I enjoyed watching how you played with those boys. It was obvious that none of them were what you needed. You, love, need a man not a boy. And I saw that you knew that and humored them at times, throwing them a bone every once in a while by letting one dance with you."

I sit my wine glass down on the table and begin to slink my way over Marco's body. He glints his eyes at me as his mouth turns up in a seductive grin.

"And you, sir, I love that controlling, dominant alpha male in you. It makes my blood run hot and sucks the air from my body."

His eyes glint seductively at me and after a moment he quietly says, "I wonder how much dominance you would actually love, Elizabeth?"

My breath catches and my body heat spikes. I stretch my body over his, sink my hands into his hair and kiss him as if I were trying to breathe him into me. When we come up for air we're panting with our desires newly ignited.

"Come on, baby, I want to take a bath with you." He stands pulling me up with him.

We take turns washing each other in the tub, resting back to front, in a long leisurely soak taking our time exploring our bodies. Each nook and curve, each crevice and fold, burning the unseen images in our minds through the sight of our hands, lips and tongues. When the water chills we getting out and dry each other, not able to keep our hands off one another.

Marco leads me to the bedroom. While our tongues are making love to each other he pulls down the comforter and guides us onto the bed and covers our naked bodies. Our limbs are entwined, our bodies not able to get close enough. The exploration continues, tasting and caressing each other from head to toe. And when he enters me and rides me through the galaxies I'm soaring and explode with the stars and never want to come down.

Afterwards I lie satisfied in his arms, so content and peaceful.

He whispers in my ear, "Feel good, baby?"

"Mmmmmmmm."

"Inside and out?"

"Mmmhmmmmmmm. You?"

"Yes, I haven't felt this way in a very long time, Elizabeth."

"Me too, Marco."

He turns me to face him in his arms as he covers my face and lips with light kisses.

"Elizabeth, there's something about you...," my heart feels like it stops, "just the thought of you arouses me. I want you but more than just your body. The hunger is so deep, it's like I crave you. I want to fill myself with you, have you running through my veins. I need to have you completely. Can you give me that, Elizabeth, can you give yourself to me?"

I know I'm not breathing, time must have stopped right here in this moment. His hands are holding my face not letting me go, forcing me to remain fixed in this spot as he's pulling me into him and I want to dive head first surrendering completely to him, body, mind and soul.

"Marco..." His name is a whisper as it leaves my

lips.

He waits silently giving me time, holding me just like that.

"There is no one else I could ever give myself to...only you." The words are true. I know I have cheated him with my answer, not telling him if I will or won't, just that I could. And I see in his eyes that he realizes that I haven't answered him completely but he takes what I can only give him right at the moment. It's only a matter of time now before the past comes back for revenge, it always comes back to haunt you.

Hesitantly he says, "I have to leave in the morning. I have a breakfast meeting. I wish I could change it but we're on a schedule."

Disappointment seeps through me as the tender moment passes and the thought of not having him with me when I wake up.

"I'll miss you but we have lives that don't stop. It's been a fantastic few days. Thank you." He has his arms wrapped around me as I'm stroking his chiseled chest.

"You can't get rid of me that easily, Elizabeth. You will let down your guards and let me in. Sooner than you think, my love," he says kissing the tip of my nose.

He doesn't realize that I've already torn them down and thrown out the bricks. But there's still a pile of rubble hiding in the background that I'm buried under, my fingers raw from trying to dig myself out. He's entered into my very soul, his light brightening the darkness inside of me. I'm trying to get to him but I can't.

I turn, snuggling to him, my back into his chest so his heartbeat vibrates against my back, enveloping me in his warmth. We talk until the early hours of the morning about nothing and everything until our eyes are burning and our mouths are dry. And the only thing I can think of is the Aerosmith song, Don't Want to Miss a Thing.

When I wake up in the morning I'm alone. I look over at the clock, it says 8:00. I roll over to his side of the bed and breathe in deeply trying to fill myself with his scent. I miss him, body, mind and soul.

Chapter 7

The agency I work for could be classified as a 'boutique agency' which is unusual for the insurance industry. We cater to the higher-end homeowner offering them an atmosphere which they are accustomed to being in while catering to all of their needs. It is posh and modern with a vintage twist and very upscale with deco furniture set in lovely Victorian details and embellishments. It's on one of the most beautiful streets of Wilmington in a smaller historic mansion. Monday morning came around too fast. I have an appointment this afternoon with a couple who just purchased a new home in the exclusive Landfall community. I'm finishing up the quotes I'm preparing for them when I get a text from Marco.

Hi baby. I hope your day is good and you're thinking of me. (I smile)*, I'm having a shitty morning. Call me when you get a chance and make me smile. M*

We had a nice conversation last night and he'd asked me if I wanted to go out to dinner with him but I made an excuse that I had to catch up on some things before the week started. I needed some time to try and sort out my feelings for him. Was it just sexual? And if it was I wanted to focus on that. But I would be lying to myself if I didn't admit that it was more. He makes me feel alive, appreciated and wanted. I think about him all the time, I miss him from deep down inside myself. And when I blew him off last night the pain I felt was heard in the disappointment in his voice when he said he understood. But to be honest I don't know what he wants or expects from me, if anything. I still have that nagging quiet little voice telling me there is something about him that's he's not telling me, a secret of his own. When I leave for lunch I've forgotten about the secret I think he's hiding and I give him a call.

"Hi baby!" He genuinely sounds happy to hear from me.

"Hi yourself. What are you wearing?" It's so good to hear his voice.

He laughs, "I'm wearing a light blue shirt and dark grey slacks. What about you?"

"A black pencil dress and heels."

"And?"

Giggling I ask, "And what?"

"What's underneath?"

"Pink bra and lace panties."

"You made me smile. But no matter what you

do you make me smile. Oh, I bought you present, baby."

"Marco, you didn't have to do that. Thank you. What is it?" I'm sure he can hear the giddiness in my voice. No one's bought me a present in so long that I've forgotten what it feels like to get one, the last present I received was from my father a couple of years ago. I feel excited but at the same time apprehensive, I can't imagine what it could be.

"It's a surprise. I can't wait to give it to you." He sounds just as excited as I feel.

I tease him, "Will I like it?"

"I'm sure you'll love it." His answer slides over my skin like his tongue, his deepening tone makes me tingle. I close my eyes trying to picture what it could be.

"I look forward to its presentation then. So what made your day so shitty?"

He lets out a huge sigh. "Someone hacked into my personal email account and wiped it clean. There were a lot of important contacts on there but I'm more concerned with privacy. He also installed a shit load of viruses that just about shut down the system."

Alarm bells start going off in my head as a feeling of dread washes over me. How did this happen, how could Santino have found out about Marco? There is nothing in black and white that links us together, no trails, nothing. I know it's him, this is his MO exactly.

"Elizabeth, are you there?"

"That's terrible. Do you know who it is?" I try to keep my voice calm trying not to let my anxiety show.

"No, the IT guy is taking care of it so everything should be fine. It's just a matter of transferring data now to replace what was lost and cleaning up the system."

Feeling slightly relieved I say, "Good, I'm glad you can get it taken care of easily. I'm sorry." If what is happening is what I think it is he has no idea how really sorry I am.

"You didn't do anything, no need to be sorry. It's more of a major headache, I hope, than anything else. As long as nothing else comes of it, everything will be fine."

Fuck. That is EXACTLY what I'm worried about. Santino starts his shit just like this every time. He hacks my accounts just about every other month wiping out my emails and contacts and I've even tried opening new accounts but somehow he finds out about those as well. He's hacked into my Facebook account and sent indecent photos he's taken of me while we Skyped to some of my contacts including the nurse, Collin. Collin called me as soon as he got them to let me know. He knew I was embarrassed but he only laughed and said, 'Hey, I liked them, the guy has no idea how much of a freak I am. I wanted to tell him to send me more but he blocked me.' I can't help it, I like the guy, he's real and doesn't care if anyone gets offended by it and I think it's admirable.

"This is not the best way to start a week." I try to continue my casual tone.

"Yes, but envisioning you in those panties and bra in your stockings and heels takes my mind off all of that. I'm getting hard just thinking about you, baby, and it's not the first time I've gotten hard thinking about you, imagining you lying on my desk and all of the things I'd like to do to you. You're going to have to come visit me at my office and let me kiss your lips on my desk before I bury myself inside of you." I can hear his arousal in his voice.

The image flashes in my mind of me open wide for him on his desk as he does exactly what he said. The heat of desire makes my groin pulse and I catch my breath.

He hears it. "You're getting wet, Elizabeth. I want to come and fuck you hard and fast right now." His voice is low and gravelly with need.

"I can't, Marco." My emotions are so conflicted the words come out in a creak.

"Oh?" He's shocked, I can hear it.

Shit. I need space. I need time apart from him to figure out what's happening and I can't do that with him seducing me and me wanting him to. I should have never let myself get in this far, I am so stupid. If it's Santino, I know I'll hear from him very soon, that's his pattern. If nothing else, he's predictable. Every time it's the same thing. He hacks, sends emails, then I cut things off and he stops. He's terrorizing me, and I let him. Why? Why have I continued to feed into this abusive cycle? I keep telling myself it's my fault, I did this to him, I made everything happen. And I keep myself in the same position still giving him control over me.

Searching for a good excuse I say, "I have a meeting with some clients that I've been preparing for. It could be a big account." It's true but he doesn't know I have two hours until I sit down with them.

"Then I guess I'll have to wait." There is a pause. "Elizabeth?"

"Yes, Marco?" I have to get away, I feel the panic beginning to rise in me.

"I missed you yesterday. And this morning. And now."

"I miss you, too, Marco." I scrunch my eyes together as my fingers go to my temples trying to stop the feeling of a stress migraine rearing its ugly head. It's the same reaction every time.

"I have to go, Marco. I hope the rest of your day is better. Bye."

"What is it, Elizabeth?"

"Nothing, why?" Please, just let me go, I hate lying.

"Don't give me that shit, I can read you like a book. What the fuck is wrong?" His arousal has turned into frustration because he knows I'm lying.

The breath I didn't know I was holding comes out heavy. "Nothing is wrong. I just have to go." I need to get him at a distance, both figuratively and physically, and keep him there.

"Don't lie to me. Tell me now." His voice is stern and I can hear his anger. He knows what I'm doing and it hurts him.

"There's nothing to tell, Marco. I'll talk to you later, have a good afternoon." I hang up. I can picture him staring at the phone being totally pissed off and wanting to throw it against the wall. I wonder if he does. Shit, I should never have let it get this far. Now he's been dragged into my mess. I was a fool to think I had time.

Its 4:00 and I'm beginning to relax. The meeting with the new clients went well, better than I could have hoped for considering what a ball of nerves I was after finding out Santino knows about Marco and worrying about what's coming next. I'd started to rationalize things by telling myself, 'This could be a complete coincidence and I'm worrying for nothing'. My phone dings with a new message. Nervousness starts to fill me but I push it aside thinking, 'It's probably Janie for yoga tonight'. I open the message and am instantly sucked into a bottomless vortex spiraling into hysteria.

Hi baby. Been having a lot of fun lately after you ruined my life? I warned you and you didn't listen. This was only the beginning, you fucking whore. I'm going to destroy you like you did me.

Panic floods me. How could Santino find out? There was nothing that could lead me to Marco. My mind is on overdrive thinking of how to stop anything more he can do and trying to figure out what he's going to do next. How did he find out? I'd never let things get to this point with anyone else after Santino so I don't have a situation to compare it to. If he truly knows everything about Marco and me Santino is capable of anything. This thing with Marco ends now. Not only to protect myself but Marco even more.

I'm worthless as tits on a man the last hour at work. Carol pokes her head in my office and asks me, "Everything alright, sugar?"

I plaster a fake smile on my face and answer brightly, "Absolutely, just happy about the appointment this afternoon."

She smiles tentatively, "Yes, that was excellent, you did good, kid. But I think you're full of crap. I'm here when you're ready to talk. Go home, kiddo." And she saunters out. Suddenly I'm jealous of her, jealous of her normal life and being able to go home to her husband who obviously adores her, jealous of being able to enjoy the good and bad in a normal relationship. I watch her leave, hoping it doesn't get to a point I do need someone to talk to.

Chapter 8

Marco's left me two messages by the time I walk into the yoga studio at 6:50. I didn't call Janie. I need this time alone to unwind and clear my head and calm down. Yoga is the best thing I can do to accomplish that. I need to get a grip on everything that is beginning to spiral out of control and figure out how to stop it before it explodes.

Call me Elizabeth 5:30

Something is wrong, talk to me 6:00

There's two more by the time I leave the studio at 8:00.

Please talk to me 7:00

Did I do something? Talk to me 7:30

My heart is breaking but I have to do this. I can't see him anymore.

When I get home I text him. I'm such a coward I can't even call him and do this.

It's been great Marco. But it's over.

If that's not cold then I don't know what is. My phone rings immediately. Knowing it's better to get this over with now rather than prolonging it any further, I answer the call.

"Hi Marco." I try to keep any emotion from my voice and hide my breaking heart. No, my heart is being ripped out of my chest but I'm kept alive so I can feel every excruciating facet of the pain that consumes me.

"What the fuck do you mean it's over?" He is irate and has every right to be. We have been lovers, intimate in the most beautiful way. He's not an idiot and knows everything that has happened is related.

"It's over Marco, I don't want to see you anymore." I'm such a lying sack of shit.

He sighs heavily, probably trying to control his anger. "I don't know what's going on here, Elizabeth." I can hear the rage simmering below his calm even tone. "It's seems like it has something to do with what happened with my computer this morning but you need to tell me. I deserve that much."

My shoulders hunch in defeat. "Marco, you deserve so much more than that and you definitely don't deserve the package that is me. So let's cut this off now before either one of us has too much invested."

"It's a little too fucking late for that, Elizabeth, and you know it!"

I cringe at the force of emotion in his voice.

He sighs trying to control himself again.

"Look, I'm sorry for yelling it's just your making me crazy. I don't know what's going on, my day has gone from bad to fucking hell just like that and I don't know why. Let me come over and we can talk, just talk if that's all you want."

That's not all I want. I want all of him. Now and for as many tomorrows as I can get. But I have to stop this and I have to let him go to make that happen. Before fixing it becomes impossible.

"No, Marco. And please…stop calling me." There goes the final twist of the knife in my heart and it hurts. I have to hold back a sob.

There's silence. I listen to his breathing as my heart is being wrenched from my chest. This man I could love happily, worshipping him beyond my last my breath. And I know that I will, no matter what.

"You don't mean that, Elizabeth." The anger in his voice has been replaced by pain because he knows I'm continuing to lie to him and that is unforgiveable.

I exhale sharply trying to grasp the last bit of my strength.

"Yes, I do. Be well, Marco. You are an amazing man. And thank you, you don't know all that you've done for me. Bye." The last word is a whisper as I hang up. I clench the phone in my hand as the sobs wrack my body and grief pummels me.

I am a zombie the rest of the week just going through the motions. The world has lost its color and it seems like it's covered in a gray dismal hue. I rely on outer forces to help me function moment by moment. I did do something productive and called a lawyer although it's probably too late to salvage what could have been between Marco and I. Sometimes the greatest sadness is for things that never were rather than what was lost.

I decide it's time to make a weekend trip to my brother's house in the mountains. Being with his kids is just the distraction I need and comfort to my broken heart. I haven't heard from Marco at all. Why should I? I told him to stop calling me. He's not a man that lowers himself to begging. And I insulted him by not being honest. I just couldn't, I was too humiliated.

Once I exit off I40 the scenery changes from the flat straight roads of the coastal area to one of rolling hills with smooth winding curves. I'm not far enough into the mountains and it's still too early in the season to see the brilliant reds from the changing of fall foliage but the roads are lined with mixes of golds and greens. Cyclones of dried leaves swirl suspended in one spot as if they are a living entity. I watch the dance, almost expecting it to take flight like a flock of birds. I affectionately call this place Redneckville. Every few miles there are homemade signs on the roadside that vary from

'Jesus is coming' to 'Deer corn for sale.' This place used to have a lot of manufacturing but that died a tragic death once it was moved overseas. Now I think the Pepsi Cola and Philip Morris plants are the only things that keep the area alive, drinking and drugs being favorite past times of a lot of locals. But it's beautiful here reminding me a lot of where my brother and I grew up, a big difference is here they have the red clay dirt like in Gone With the Wind and ours was just plain brown.

I come out of the shower at my brother Rays house in sweat pants and a sweat shirt, my lips a little blue.

"Jesus, Ray, You still haven't fixed that hot water heater?!" I don't know if they have a burnt out element or if the tank's too small but the hot water dies about 5 to 10 minutes into a shower. Not the best thing to experience first thing in the morning.

Ray looks at me with an embarrassed boyish smile.

"Hahahaha! Freeze your ass off, Liz?"

"You're the ass! Sometimes I think you get some kind of sick satisfaction from that." I glint my eyes at him feigning annoyance.

"It *is* funny. But I've been so busy with finishing Alexis' room and everything else.......I guess I forgot about it. It's always been like that so it's normal to us," he finishes, shrugging his shoulders.

This is what a normal life is supposed to be, dysfunctional, crazy, busy, but love and family. Melancholy tries to seep in but I refuse to let it, I won't let it threaten my few days of escape from its ever present company.

"How are things anyway, bro?" I sit and join him at the farm style table in front of the huge window overlooking the backyard and trampoline. My hands wrap around my cup of tea as we have a brief moment of closeness between us, I take advantage of these infrequent times of just him and me.

"Good. You know, I still hate my job but everything's good." His smile and lack of words speak volumes.

"Yeah, I know," I say as both of us drift off in our minds to what our own visions of happily ever after was supposed to be. No one warned us what being a grown-up was really like although our childhood would not have been considered normal by most people.

He's turning his coffee cup in his hands as the playfulness leaves his face.

"Santino contacted me." It's almost a whisper and I see the discomfort in his expression.

"You're kidding me? I'm sorry he bothered you, Ray." Guilt fills me again.

"No, don't, it's no big deal." He slowly lifts his gaze to me with questions in his eyes. "Is he still here, Liz?"

My jaw drops at the absurdity of the question. He has no idea of what went on during Santino's time here, just what happened between Adrianna and my dad. When I was in my hell and I needed someone to help me he turned his back on me, cutting me out. It's only recently we've been able to get back that closeness we shared growing up, the two of us inseparable a lot of the times. Even when we were young adults we confided in each other, spending nights getting drunk and joking around. One night in particular sticks out in my mind about a lamp of a sailor, we called him Ahab, coming to life and killing us in our sleep. We scared the shit at of ourselves so badly we had to get rid of the lamp in our drunken stupor that night. It was about 2:00 AM and we were arguing on where to dump it, that memory still makes me laugh to this day.

"Of course he's not! Damn, Ray, what does everyone think? That I've got him locked away somewhere and I take him out to play with him whenever I want?"

He can't help but laugh at that.

"I'm sorry, I know. But that guy is a master of manipulation," and looking right into my face he continues, "and you know it."

I let out a heavy sigh, struggling with my own thoughts. "Yes, I know that better than any of you ever will. But you've got to be open with me so I can feel safe knowing I can trust you."

"Common Liz, you know that you can with anything. The past is the past and we have to leave it there. I just ignored him, not giving him the satisfaction of letting him think that anything he had to say was of any importance." He lays his hand on mine, a comforting gesture, making me feel secure. Something I needed.

"Daddy, the boys took my Kindle and won't tell me where it is!" Alexis tiny little girl voice comes from around corner before she does.

Alexis is Rays youngest child and she's got him wrapped around her little finger, truly daddy's little princess. She comes into the kitchen and squirms up on his lap with her bedhead and pouty lips.

"Alright, baby, let's go take care of those mean big brothers of yours."

I can't help but smile at the innocent scene of power play between a daughter and her father, my heart breaking for something so powerfully beautiful that I'm sure I'll never have.

The weekend helped with my brother and his family. I love the fall air up there and children always bring life to the walking dead. When I get home to my apartment the quiet and solitude that I usually relish falls heavily on me like a prison door.

Tuesday I'm still in mourning. I've barely eaten anything and I can't stop crying and it shows in my swollen eyes. I sleep for shit and it makes me look hollow and gaunt, although makeup helps a little but it can't put life back into my eyes. Carol has tried to coax me into telling her what's wrong, even our little game doesn't make me laugh anymore. Sometimes the mundane is a precious gift. It lends to normalcy forcing one to participate in this thing called life. Life. The thing that we experience on a day to day basis, getting up, doing what we do during the day, paying bills, eating, sleeping. If it wasn't for the sun and the clock, I would be lost.

About 11:00 I hear the alert that someone has walked into the office so I get up to greet them.

"Elizabeth." It's Marco. His voice is a whisper but I hear him as if his lips said the word close to my ear. Nothing exists but us, there is no time, no right, no wrong, reality and fantasy are one. I watch breathless the shifting of emotions from shocked to confusion to joy in that face I've missed so much. I stare at him not believing what I'm seeing. Just the sight of him is like breathing life into me. I have been numb, non-existent since the last time I was with him, until now.

"What are you doing here, Marco?" The question comes out barely audible.

"This is Marco?" I hear Carol's voice behind me and I turn as Marco's gaze slowly shifts from me to her.

What I want to do is go to him, wrap myself around him, absorb him into me, fill all of my senses with him but I try to regain my composure. "Yes, Carole, this is Marco Kastanopoulis." Turning back to Marco I make the formal introductions. "This is Carol Williams, senior agent here." The words come out of my mouth mechanically but in my head I'm saying, 'I am alive again just by the sight of him, just from being in his presence. How did I get so lucky to be able to see him again?'

Marco extends his hand to her. "It's a pleasure to meet you." His eyes return to me soaking me in.

Even in his tailored navy pinstriped suit that defines his beautiful body I see that he looks tired and hasn't shaved in a few days, his beard and moustache are longer than usual. Looking closer at him I see the suit is a little loose and his cheeks look sunken as if he's lost some weight. That knife is twisting back in my gut.

"It's very nice to meet you as well. Elizabeth has spoken of you."

His face brightens and he smiles quirking an eyebrow at me. I smile back at him, I can't help it, it's so good to see him

"That is very good to hear." He looks at me like, 'I knew you were full of shit.'

There is a pause in our conversation as Marco and I just take each other in, filling ourselves as if we were the food we have been starved of these past days. We've forgotten that Carol's there and we come back to the reality when she finally breaks the moment.

"Is there something we can help you with today, Marco?"

"Yes, thank you, I'm a real estate developer, my

group MKD Enterprises and I will begin work on property below the bridge which will consist of residential and commercial properties."

"I've read about your project, it was in the newspaper. It looks very impressive, Marco." It shows Carol obviously admires what she knows about the project Marco and his company have planned. I feel inept due to my lack of interest in anything that has to do with news. My life under a rock includes everything worldly and that is glaringly rearing its ugly head right now.

Marco appears to be proud and shy at the same time being on the receiving end of praise.

"Thank you. Our goal is to bring environmentally conscious technology to grass roots America for everyone's benefit, today and tomorrow. Beauty does not have to come with a high price tag." His passion and commitment to his work is genuine, truly a part of him.

"I know of a lot of people, some who will be very good people to have on your side, that feel the same way." Carol is very popular with a lot of individuals and the way she silently works her charm could be utilized in the right way. It seems she has just given her allegiance to Mr. Sexy Kastanopoulis.

"I sincerely appreciate that, Carol. These ideals are not considered 'hippy' thinking anymore but necessary for human sustainability."

My regard for this man has just shot through the roof and my heart swells with pride for him.

"I'd like to talk with you about my needs," he says looking straight into my eyes. "You are exactly what I need to take care of them."

Carol clears her throat. "Well, I'm sure Elizabeth is more than happy to take care of you," she says and pokes me in the back making me jump. "I'll just leave you two discuss the details and you're specifics." She walks away leaving us, giggling as she goes.

"Why don't we go into my office so we can talk about your project," I say trying to focus but thinking, 'So I can fantasize about you taking me on my desk like you said you would before.'

"Let's go, Elizabeth." Those famous three words that started it all still affect me the same way as they did then and make me flush.

I sit and he takes a seat across from me, sitting back in that casual authoritative way, resting an ankle on his knee with his arms lying comfortably on the armrests. I lean forward and take a pen in my hand playing with it, mostly for something to do to relieve the nerves that have settled in.

"So, a real estate developer, huh?" I smirk at him.

"Yep. And you a rep in a boutique agency. It suits you." His smile is warming and affectionate. I love the way it touches my heart and hate the guilt I feel for not being open with him.

"Well, thank you, as does yours. But it appears you are much more than that. Been chewing them up and spitting them out lately, Mr. Bond?"

He throws his head back and laughs. God, how I've missed that sound.

"No, I haven't really had the desire. I believe it was me who was chewed up and spit out, Miss DiStefano," he replies, becoming serious.

I sit back and lower my gaze to hide the hurt in my face. I deserved that and more.

He leans forward and quietly says to me, "I'm sorry. I shouldn't have said that. How've you been, Elizabeth? I hate to say it but you don't look as beautiful as you usually do, exactly how I feel."

"Let's not discuss it, Marco." I push the words past the rock that has embedded in my throat. I can't do this now, especially not here.

"It's obvious, Elizabeth. We need to discuss it." Frustration flares in his face but his body is still in control.

"Now is not the time or place, Marco. Tell me about your development and what you would like for us to do and maybe I can give you some suggestions on some other ways we can help you." I steer the conversation to business and try to attempt to keep the mood light.

"Alright." His expression tells me that he'll let it go...for now.

I reach over and put on my reading glasses and look up at him a little embarrassed.

"So now you know I'm really a geek," I smile

shyly at him.

"On the contrary, you are even sexier like this, if that's possible." The desire is evident in his voice.

He sits back and outlines the plans for the residential and commercial units and the building timelines. I take notes and add how we can work with his company beyond the initial upfitting by communicating with the prospective homeowners in answering their questions during open houses and informational seminars. We put some things together to fill his immediate needs and I tell him that I will get back to him with a prospectus to coordinate with his timeline.

The business discussion has come to an end and an awkward silence falls showing that neither of us wants this to be done. I rise slowly and he follows my movement. I extend my hand to shake his to thank him for the opportunity in working with him. But I don't want him to leave. What I want to do is grovel at his feet, tell him how sorry I am and that I didn't mean any of the things I said. And mostly, please help me get out of this mess so I can belong to you. But I don't say any of those things and just try to keep the pleading look out of my eyes.

He holds my outstretched hand in both of his larger ones. I love his hands, so strong, so competent, I love the veins in them showing the fact that he has lived life and it has made him who he is. "Walk me to my car, Elizabeth," the subtle command tinging his words makes my heart swell. I'm singing 'Alleluia' inside as my eyes search his face. I just can't let him go yet. I crave him, all of him, his presence, his smile, his warmth, everything.

"Ok. Just a second," and I see my relief reflected in his eyes.

I sit to send Carol an IM.

I'm going to walk Marco to his car.

It's almost lunchtime. Why don't you go with him? He looks like he needs nourishment. ☺ Suits a little loose. She noticed it too. God, this woman is the best.

I bite my lip, do I suggest it?

"Join me for lunch. We've got to eat, it looks like neither of us have been doing much of that lately. It'll be a business lunch." It's not a request. He's telling me that he will not be played with but on my terms.

He had me at 'lunch'.

"Ok, I'd planned on going after we finished." And I'm saying, 'I'm not playing with you, just doing what I've got to.'

"Well, timing is everything." He doesn't buy it, sweet sarcasm dripping from his voice.

Going to lunch.

Have fun ;)

:p

I get my bag and sweater and say to him with a mischievous smile, "Let's go, Marco." He so totally got it and it shows in that wicked smile of his.

He leads me out in that delicious way he does with his hand on the small of my back making me swoon. I absolutely cannot resist this man at all. But I have to stay strong. 'Don't dive back in, Elizabeth.' I repeat this over and over again in my head with everything in me pushing me in the opposite direction right into his arms.

We go to Front Street Brewery, all polished brass and heavily lacquered wood, the place filled with the usual crowd of artificial people with over inflated egos, everyone trying to appear as if they're someone important. Why is that? Why must we categorize ourselves into a slot of 'so-called somebody' when it's really all just bullshit anyway?

I don't know anything about micro-brewing but they do that here. We pass the big brass brewer things in the front of the restaurant enclosed in a room full of windows with black and white plaques labelling the contents inside the huge urn like structures. The cute hostess leads us to a corner table upstairs smiling shyly at Marco. What is it and this guy always getting us secluded tables? He's got some kind of a knack.

"I'm starving," he says as we're glancing over the menu looking up at me.

"Me too!" and we both laugh. But the laughter dies and is replaced with longing. I have to look away because what I really want is so obvious, it's written all over my face and body. In the way my eyes eat him up, the way my chest rises and falls, how my lips part just thinking of the feel of his mouth on mine remembering the way it claims all of me.

The waitress is a young attractive college age girl with large perky breasts and a tight very round bottom dressed in the black t-shirt and yoga pant unofficial uniform. When she bends down her boobs practically are in Marco's face, (are you kidding me?), pointing to the special items and the seasonal beers on the menu, todays 'Mug of the Day' is Amberjack. But he barely looks at her, his eyes never leaving me. She brings our drinks and he orders for us both, the grilled chicken sandwich with sweet potato fries for me and the black and blue burger with fries for himself.

"It was really a nice surprise to see you today, Elizabeth." His tone is sincere and affectionate.

I smile, shaking my head, remembering my shock in seeing him standing in the office. "Yes, it was."

He takes my hand across the table and strokes my knuckles lightly.

"When are you going to tell me what's going on?" he asks quietly but firmly.

I lower my head. And I lie...again. "There's nothing going on, Marco." I can't look him in the eye because he can see right through me, holding me open and dissecting me bit by bit. That will only confirm what he already knows, that I am blatantly withholding the truth from him.

"That's bullshit, Elizabeth."

I look up at him, determined to change the topic but not pulling my hand away, relishing his touch. "So, what you got into in Florida after you left New York was real estate?"

He puts his head down and laughs, "You're changing the subject. But, yes, it was. I enjoy creating beautiful things. It's a bit like art. You have an idea and you watch it grow and come to life as each part is built piece by piece. And this is an especially great project because of the kind of area where it's going. I'm very glad I found Wilmington and plan on being here a while."

There is so much more to that statement than what is on the surface and it warms me inside. I silently hope that I can be a part of that in the future. But I know I can't right now. I think he can see this on my face because his genuine smile says he hopes the same thing.

I tell him about my weekend at my brothers and how his kids kicked my butt in video games. He laughs hard.

Cocking his head to the side he states rather than asks, "You like kids."

Blushing and shrugging my shoulders slightly I say quietly, "Yeah, I do. I like them better than adults. How can you tell?"

His smile is appreciative. "By the way you talk about your brothers kids."

"I love them like they are my own. I love all of

my nieces and nephews like that. I'm god mother to three of them." Smiling at a special memory I continue, "My brother Rays oldest boy and I have this little secret," and I lean in as if divulging important information, "he says I'm his favorite aunt but can't tell anyone because he doesn't want to hurt anyone's feelings." My smile practically breaks my face.

"You're going to be a wonderful mother, Elizabeth."

I'm embarrassed at his tender thought but I think that's never going to happen. "Thank you."

He tells me he spent the weekend working and looking for a place to move to in order to get out of the hotel. Our food comes and we naturally begin our familiar way of sharing a meal, tasting each other's food and wiping the corners of our mouths as we've done so many times. In such a short period we have so much history between us of moments shared and memories we've made. We're so comfortable together, it's like I'm swimming against the current trying to resist him and it's so hard, fighting this thing between us.

When he takes me back to the office he doesn't get out of the car. Instead he grabs my arm as I'm opening the door.

"Wait."

I turn and look at him expectantly.

His hand is on the back of my head in my hair bringing my face to his.

"God, Elizabeth, seeing you today was like the elixir of life for me."

I search his eyes as his breath warms my lips, he's so close.

"Me too, Marco...."

He kisses me as if I am his sustenance, deep and hard, his tongue licking and tasting and savoring mine. He bites my lip, sucking it softly between his. I have missed his mouth so much and I return the passion of his kiss. He's feasting on my mouth as I am his and its spectacular.

We're breathless as he holds my face close to his, our foreheads pressed gently against each other.

"I have to go, Marco...."

"I know...," and he kisses me lightly on my forehead, then my nose, then my lips, his lips nipping each place.

I lift my head and look into his eyes seeing my burning hunger looking back at me.

"Bye......"

"Bye......"

There are no promises, no requests. Nothing needs to be spoken out loud because we know what the other wants. And what we can or can't give.

Chapter 9

Marco and I haven't spoken again this week but he sent me a text late Tuesday.

I just wanted to take a moment to say thank you for sitting down with me and discussing my needs. Gratefully yours, Marco

I warm with the unsaid meaning of his words. I want to fulfill all of his needs, on my back, on all fours, on my knees, in the shower, it doesn't matter.

I was very happy to do it and I'm looking forward to a long successful relationship. Sincerely, ~Elizabeth

I'm nervous because of the real meaning behind my reply and I hope he will understand that and I hope that once all of this is behind me he will still want me.

As am I and I'm sure once the preliminaries have been taken care of we will enjoy the fruits of our labor. Diligently, Marco

The preliminaries are already underway and I

*will keep you abreast of their progress.
Thoroughly, Elizabeth*

*I look forward to hearing the outline of what you
have to offer. Patiently, Marco*

*I have no doubt when the time comes you will be
very pleased. Hopeful, Elizabeth*

That time can't be soon enough. Waiting, Marco

Hope fills me and I'm energized with renewed
strength. If he can give me just a little more time,
which he says he will, I'll fix all of this mess and
stop anyone else from getting hurt, me, Marco and
Santino included.

It's Friday and I'm almost dreading spending a
lonely weekend in my apartment after having
Marco's lips on me. I try my best to keep the
impending loneliness at bay knowing that once I
walk into my apartment tonight all I'll think about
is the seeing him there with me. The memories of
being with Marco this week gives me the strength to
do that. It's 3:00 and Carol calls me into her office.

"Can you come in here a minute, Elizabeth?"

Warning bells start to go off in my head because
her tone is so impersonal and I begin to sweat. Our
boss, the agency owner, is now out on maternity
leave and Carol is officially in charge assuming all
business and corporate issues.

I walk across to her office, close the door and sit
in the chair across from her. She doesn't look at
me. I don't know if she can't or won't and I
instantly know this is not good. I start to fidget with

my clothes as my nerves build. She exhales slightly and turns her gaze to me with a blank expression which only confirms it, this is more than not good, this is bad.

"Elizabeth, we all know that you have been doing a phenomenal job since you joined us."

My jaw drops.

"Am I getting fired?" I croak out.

"No! But we received a suggestive message about you."

Fuck! I cannot believe Santino, he's never stooped this low before.

"How bad was it, Carol. Tell me truth." I had to know.

She steals herself and begins, "It suggested that you participate in unscrupulous activities both professionally and personally and it would be financially beneficial for the company and clients if you did not work here."

I feel like I have just been punched in the stomach, the pain is physical and excruciating. I cannot say a word, I am so stunned.

She continues, "Now you know we don't believe a word of it. But corporate policy is such that it must be investigated. So, with that being said corporate has asked that we run another background check and...," her words trail off not being able to verbalize the implications. She sighs.

"Go on." I can't believe my tone is as calm as it

is.

"A lie detector test."

"Are you serious?" I can't hide my astonishment.

"It's just policy due to the nature of the allegations."

"I understand. No problem." There is no emotion, no reaction in my voice and expression and I think it's because I'm in shock.

"I thought as much but of course...," she continues hesitantly.

"Yes...," I wish she'd just spit every fucking thing out, my anger is rising rapidly.

"You're business access has been suspended until all of the results are reviewed and determined. I am so sorry, Elizabeth." There is hurt and pity in her voice and it makes me cringe, I hate people feeling sorry for me.

"It's not your fault, Carol." I am officially humiliated and fucking mad as hell.

"Well, off the record then, you must have really pissed someone off and they want to get back at you badly to come at you this way," she says as her body relaxes slightly. Carol opens her desk drawer and pulls out her vapor Ecig and starts puffing on it with a cocky smirk on her face. She knows she can get away with certain things as the unofficial senior in the office. My boss would be nowhere without Carol and she knows it but she doesn't take advantage of it, except right now with the Ecig, it's a small indulgence and Carol loves it.

I sit back in the chair and roll my eyes at how right she is. I want to ask her if I can have a hit off of that, my how times have changed.

"Yeah, my ex, Santino. I might as well come clean as he's obviously made his presence very well known. That son of a bitch hacked into Marco's personal email account, wiped it clean and loaded his system with viruses on Monday. I don't know how he found out about us but he did and this is his way of pay back. Because I knew he wasn't done with his games yet, I stopped seeing Marco. That's why we were so shocked to see each other here the other day. But this," and I sweep my hand towards Carol, "is new for him." There, most of the story is out.

She lets out a low whistle, "Wow, Elizabeth. I am so sorry you have to live with this." She shakes her head with disbelief taking it all in.

"Oh, this is nothing compared to when he was here," I say thinking back to those times.

"What are you going to do? How can you stop him?"

"Well, there's one thing I can do for starters and I've already met with a lawyer about it," I say with new conviction filling me.

"Good. Let me know if there's anything I can do," and she takes my hand with compassion in her eyes, "as a friend."

"Thanks, Carol, but you've already been dragged in enough. And there's nothing you can do. So, what do I do now? Do I come into work?"

"Corporate didn't say anything about suspending you, just your access. So, continue to come in and any applications you can do hardcopy, do that way and I'll make sure you get paid for them."

"Thanks, Carol. I really appreciate it." I am so lucky because if this had to happen it happened with her on my side. I am finally feeling the strength to relieve myself of these chains of past torment I've worn willingly. It's definitely way past time I fought back.

I'm on my first glass of wine at 7:00 as I lower myself into a hot bubble bath. This is just what I needed. Well, almost. I can think of much better and he's a delicious 6' tall man with a magical mouth, tantalizing fingers and the most amazing lover I have ever known. But more than that he is an incredibly kind, patient, strong and considerate man. And I love him...because of who he is. My heart aches as my body reacts to the memories of him, how he hears the call of my yearning and answers each plea with complete perfection.

I lean my head back against the tub and sigh loudly. My world is collapsing around me, smashing everything in its wake. I know Santino's not done yet. As a matter of fact, I'm sure he's just getting started.

I put on the piano concerto Marco had on the other night when we were in this exact same place. It seems like a million years ago now. I drift back to that night and I'm reliving it in my mind when my phone rings. Looking over the edge at the caller ID, I see it's Marco and my heart skips a beat.

"Hello."

"Who the fuck is Santino really, Elizabeth?" He is so angry.

"Why? What happened, Marco?" Newly resurging dread courses through my veins at what I'm pretty sure he's talking about.

"Just tell me who the fuck he is!!!" His patience is gone with this latest event.

I try to remain calm as I sit up in the tub, the warm water splashing around me as my skin reacts to the cool air. "Please tell me what happened, Marco."

I hear his in and out breathing as he's trying to get himself under control. "He sent me some photos of you and had some lovely things to say as well. Now, tell me who he is." His words come out dragged between gritted teeth.

Oh, God! Feeling defeated, I tell him, "He's my husband."

He explodes and he has every right to. "Are you fucking kidding me?! You're married?! Why didn't you tell me, Elizabeth? Didn't you think I needed to know something like that?"

I knew this was going to happen and I probably made it worse because I didn't tell him from the beginning. I thought it was going to be a one night between us, then it turned into two, then we're cooking together. How did it get so far so fast? I saw the signs and ignored them, burying my head in the ecstasy and forgetting my reality. Now it's blowing up in my face and taking out innocent casualties because of my negligence.

"It's not like that." I let out a heavy sigh. "He's been gone over two and a half years."

"I'm on my way there and I don't want any more bullshit. You are going to tell me everything. Tonight." And he hangs up.

It's time for him to know the whole story, Santino has made sure of it. I'm grateful, actually, that everything's coming out. I have been a coward for way too long, hiding in this self-imposed prison of my life, not living, just existing. And if I'd done what I should have done two years ago all of this could have been avoided.

I get out of the tub and throw on some leggings and a t-shirt. Five minutes later the doorbell rings. I steal myself for the confrontation I know is coming and go to answer the door barefooted, my hair still up from the bath.

When I open the door my heart skips. His brow is furrowed in his residual anger, his jaw is clenched but his eyes soften when he sees me. He's in those jeans that fit him perfectly in all the right places with a white thermal and boots.

"Come in." I stand aside to let him enter. He stops once he's inside and turns to me as I walk by him.

His hand reaches up to touch the damp hair at the nape of my neck. "You were in the bath." I know he's thinking of our bath like I was, remembering the intimate closeness we shared just a few nights ago, it was much more than just physical.

"Yes, I was. With a glass of wine, would you like one? I had a shit day myself," my nonchalance is an attempt to hide my nervousness and instant reaction to him.

He looks at me trying to read me answering, "Sure."

I go into the kitchen to refill my glass and get one for Marco as he makes himself comfortable on the couch, one arm stretched along the back, the other on the armrest. I hand him his wine and take the seat in the chair. If this is a bare it all inquisition, I need some space. He sits quietly looking at me intently waiting for me to say something.

Squaring my shoulders I begin. "I guess I need to start at the beginning. All that I ask is that you please not judge me and let me finish."

"Of course, Elizabeth. I would think that you know me at least a little by now." He sits back and takes a sip of his wine listening, his mouth a thin line and his eyes focused on me.

This is going to suck.

"About four and a half years ago I met Santino on Facebook." His eyebrows raise and I put up my hand to stop his train of thought. "Remember what I asked, Marco." He nods his head in understanding. "Well, we began chatting and before I knew it I was completely intrigued by him. A few months of talking we agreed he would come to visit, he was in the UK." I look off to some place in my mind going back to that time. "When he left I had been utterly and completely seduced and enchanted by him, he seemed perfect. A man who was confident in himself and confident in being with a woman." I glance at him and I see a flash of emotion cross his face. I don't mean to hurt him but I to have tell him everything, the why's and how's. "Over the course of two years and many transatlantic flights I fell madly and deeply in love with him. He had asked me to marry him and we shopped for the ring while I was over there. We decided, or maybe he'd planned all along, I'm not sure, that he would move here. I had to get the immigration paperwork together and Janie helped me with that. She was aware of the whole relationship right from the beginning, although she doesn't know how it ended. No one knows, except now you." Again, I look at him, his face is still non-expressive. He nods as if saying, 'continue.'

"The last time I went to visit him he pushed me around a couple of times. Funny thing is it turned me on." I lower my head, shaking it, laughing quietly. "But from the beginning he would always go off on these tirades in insane attacks of anger for no apparent reason. The things he would say to me

I would never say to anyone. But I chose to ignore it, even asking him to forgive me and apologizing for the thing I must have done to cause it.

My father was still alive at that time and my sister was living with him. He had been diagnosed with cancer and after my mother died a few years earlier, Adriana had taken on the role of his 'wife', so to speak. That is another story entirely which makes me sick." I pause for a moment, thinking of it then continue, "I had spoken to them from the start about him. Obviously, they wanted to know where and why I was going on all of these trips. I told my brother and his family as well. I wanted to tell them about the man I had fallen in love with, wanting them to like him too. They were very suspicious right from the beginning. They said, 'Why would a grown man leave his home and family for a stranger'. The more I talked the more they disliked him.

He finally arrived and things were great for a few weeks. He insisted we get married immediately so we had the ceremony within a month. My father was very nice and polite, having us over for dinner frequently and stopping by to say hello. Or should I say that my sister had us over for dinner. She would stop by alone sometimes for no reason. One night at my dad's at dinner I'd left the room. She whispered in Santino's ear, 'Don't tell my sister but I love to do special things for you'. About a week after that she stopped by again, my sister doesn't wear a bra, she came in and stuck her breasts out and said, 'Look how cold it is outside'. I was speechless." I look at him with eyes wide showing how shocked I was by a woman showing her sisters man her hardened nipples. "About a week after that she called and said my dad wanted us to come for dinner. I could tell she'd been drinking but we went anyway. She became belligerent, saying things like I'd always been jealous of her then she made some comment which I don't remember to my father. He was laughing off her drunken stupidness and making jokes. She started a fight with Santino and asked him to go to her room to discuss it. He refused and told her they could talk about it in the living room. She raised her hand as if to slap him and he pushed her away. She fell. We left and shortly after that the police came because Adriana had called them. That was the first night he hit me. I couldn't go to work for a few days because of my face. The hell was non-stop after that until I put him on a plane to go back. I knew I had to find a way to get him to leave when he threatened my family. Whether or not he meant it, I don't know, but I couldn't take the chance."

I look at him again and his expression hasn't changed but there's rage in his eyes.

"Before he got on the plane he said lovingly to me," and I laugh, "that he would come back for me. But I was so glad he was gone."

I sigh and take a sip of wine. "The first year he was gone we still spoke. He was filled with anger. He told me I ruined his life, that I sent him back humiliated and he blamed me for the disaster here." I take another sip of wine.

"For a long time, pretty much until this year, I felt completely responsible and extremely guilty.

Now, the situation that had happened with Adriana caused mine and my father's relationship to stop. Regardless of what Santino was doing to me she had caused the fight that night. My father was going to disown me because of that. And all the while I was going through hell and had no one I could turn to. I felt very alone.

When my dad got very sick I went to visit him frequently and he came over for dinner by himself, we had some very special moments in the end. The guilt I carry because of our strained relationship tears me up so badly sometimes and I blame Adriana. And for that, I can never forgive her."

I look into his eyes and he looks confused.

"Why haven't you divorced him yet?"

I look up to the ceiling trying to find the words.

"I guess because of the guilt I felt for having put him in that situation. I felt completely responsible. You know, I made him come over here and give up everything."

And I stop to think of my next words. I knew I had to be completely honest.

"And I guess that I couldn't believe that a love that strong could turn into such a tragedy. It took me a long time to admit it and finally let it go in my heart."

He comes to me and takes my hand.

"He was and is completely responsible for everything. His actions before, during and after. You did nothing wrong."

"You know he did that to your computer. I don't know how he found out about us though. Only three people know about you and I. And today he sent my company false allegations about me having inappropriate conduct both professionally and privately. Now they need to do an investigation and a lie detector test and my privileges have been suspended."

"What a coward, a complete and total fucking asshole!"

"I know. But I did talk to a lawyer last week and I've started divorce proceedings."

"I'll expedite it for you so he has no legal standing whatsoever. I don't give a shit about the hacking. I just hope he's not stupid enough to mess with my contacts."

"I don't know about that."

He hesitates, looking into my eyes. "This is the reason you said you didn't want to see me anymore."

"Yes....," I answer quietly.

"You should have told me, Elizabeth."

"Everything happened so fast, Marco. And to be honest, I didn't know what this," waving my hand back and forth between us, "is between us."

He looks down and takes both my hand in his.

"Yes, everything was very fast. But what I do know is that I'm not going anywhere. I've tried staying away from you.....but I can't. Especially not now, I'm not leaving you alone. Who knows what that crazy son of a bitch will do next." His face turns to mine. "You're not getting rid of me again." Sitting up he pulls gently on my hand, "Common, come sit with me."

I stand, moving towards him as he slides back down to his end of the couch bringing me down next to him.

"Come, lay down and put your head on my lap, baby."

I take his invitation both hesitantly and eagerly. Gently letting my hair down, running his fingers through it, his gentle touch is a balm to my soul, each stroke easing a frayed nerve one at a time.

"It kills me, Elizabeth that you had to live through that. But what's worse is that he is still terrorizing you. He doesn't have the courage to be a man."

"Let's not talk about him anymore. He's taken so much time from me and I don't want to waste anymore."

"You're right, baby," and he lowers his face to mine, kissing me softly. With his lips close to mine, his fingertips stroking my cheek, he whispers, "I've missed you, Elizabeth. A lot."

"Me too, Marco." I lift my arms and pull his lips down to mine and kiss him with the passion that I feel for him.

"I want to make love to you."

"Yes, please...," it comes out almost as begging.

"Let's go to bed, baby."

I stand and pull him to me. Removing each other's clothes slowly and leaving a trail on the way to the bedroom, our hands stroke and kiss the flesh as it is exposed, showering it with appreciation like precious gifts, each part adored. Pulling the comforter down, he guides me onto the bed, never breaking our kiss. Our hands are moving over our bodies in slow motion, burning a trail in their wake setting fire to our skin. His mouth consumes my breasts with a smoldering hunger. I take his hardness into my mouth needing to savor the taste of him on my tongue. His fingers are inside of, me loving me there. Then his mouth laps my juices devouring each drop. Our lovemaking is sensual, taking our time, rediscovering our bodies with a thoroughness of lovers that have been apart too long. He enters me slowly and I love the feel of every inch of him filling me. He is consuming me completely and we ride the ecstasy with each trust into bliss.

As we lay there still on our high, I sigh with contentment. Our limbs are entwined tying us together.

"When we get this behind us, Elizabeth, there aren't going to be anymore secrets." His words are soft but the intent is clear.

"No, Marco, no more." And for once I feel hope, something I haven't felt in a long time. But there is still a little nagging feeling at the back of my mind of something about him that I don't know about. I know he's referring to me not keeping secrets from him so I let it go. For now.

My stomach makes a gurgling noise and his hand reaches down to caress it as he smiles.

"You haven't eaten tonight, have you?"

"Um, no, I wasn't in much of a mood for food, but you haven't either, have you?"

And his stomach growls as if to answer.

"I guess not, huh?" He laughs. "Common, I think I can find something for us to eat."

He gets out of bed and pulls on his boxers, (I'll never get enough of that sight), and hands me my robe. We hold hands as we walk into the kitchen.

"Sit," he says, kissing me gently, and begins to put together a snack. He is so in control, he knows exactly what needs to be done and does it and it makes me feel safe.

As we're sitting down eating, Marco is stroking my thigh as he gently traces his fingers up the inside, across the edge of my thigh, and down the outer skin. I play with my food as anxiety begins to rise in me again.

"What's wrong, Elizabeth?" He asks laying his palm on my leg trying to calm me.

I look up at him and take a deep breath.

"You know, you don't have to babysit me. This is my mess and I never wanted anyone else to get sucked in."

"Are you serious? Do you honestly think I'm here because I'm babysitting you?" He sits back in his chair with a look of disbelief on his face.

Shit, I can tell I've insulted him again. I have an incredible gift of screwing things up.

"I'm sorry. I don't mean to insult you but I don't want you to feel responsible for me."

"You're damn right I feel responsible for you. You're mine now, Elizabeth, and the sooner you accept that and stop pushing me away, the easier it's going to be for both of us." He comes in closer, intense emotion in his eyes. "Listen to me very carefully. I hate that I wasn't the one you met four years ago. I hate that it was him you fell deeply in love with and worshipped. And I especially hate the fact he ripped that love and adoration to shreds, beating you, tearing you into a million pieces. If I could, I would tear all of that from you and erase that completely from your soul to take your pain away." He looks deeply into my eyes as they fill with tears. "But I can't. What I can do is help you heal, replace all of that shit with everything I can give you, adore you as you give yourself to me."

He wraps his hand around the back of my neck bringing his mouth down hard on mine, branding me, claiming me with his searing kiss, shoving his tongue so deep in my mouth I feel it in my heart.

Pulling his face slightly away from mine as tears stream down my face and he wipes them gently away, saying in a gentle voice, "Don't cry, love, I'm here now and I'll take care of you.

"Thank you," the words come out choked. And all the years of holding things in, hiding behind the walls I've built up, everything comes crumbling down and in that instant I give myself to him, heart, body, and soul.

He takes me in his arms, kissing the tears away and takes me back to bed. He holds me close until the sobbing subsides and I'm finally ready to move on, the burden of guilt now gone.

I'm a sniffling mess, wiping my nose on the back of my hand. He gets up and returns with a handful of tissues and hands them to me. We laugh, both of us feeling lighter. He settles back in bed, wrapping himself around me and rests my bottom against his groin.

"Sleep now, baby," he whispers in my ear sucking the lobe between his lips.

And for the first time in years I feel completely and utterly calm and safe.

I wake in the morning to an empty bed and the murmured sound of Marco's voice coming from the main rooms. I can tell he's agitated. I get up and go to the bathroom to fix the bedhead mess that I am. Going to the kitchen I walk in quietly not wanting to disturb him. I make his coffee and my tea and hand him his cup. He mouths, 'Thank you, baby,' and puckers his lips asking for a kiss and I answer giving it to him.

"What the fuck?! I thought we had more than sufficient security measures in place?! Some insignificant piece of shit hacker shouldn't be able to break into our stuff!" He's yelling into the phone.

A pause.

"I don't want to hear about IP addresses! Just get it fixed. NOW!" Click.

Silence hangs heavy like a pregnant hippopotamus as we look at each other, Marco with a seething expression, me worried chewing on my thumbnail. I don't want to know the details. I already know its Santino.

He shoves himself from his seat and begins pacing the room with frustration pouring off of him. He's dressed just in his jeans and his skin glows with the flexing of his muscles rippling below the surface. He is still sexy as fucking hell.

"Piece of fucking shit!! I would love the opportunity to beat the shit out of him!"

I don't say anything because I know I need to give him time to calm down. But I can't help envisioning Marco as a bad ass. I can definitely see it and it is arousing, a bad boy in a nice suit.

He walks the room a few times as I watch him decompress. Whew. He comes over to me and grabs me by my hand and takes me to the couch pulling me down on his lap and buries his face in my throat breathing deeply and squeezing me tight.

"Good morning, baby," he breathes out heavily.

I shove my hands in his hair grabbing fistfuls.

"Good morning," I say softly into the top of his head.

"I have some things to take care of, as I'm sure you heard. I'll be a little while."

I kiss his hair.

"Ok, I'll take a shower and fix us breakfast." He sucks the flesh of my neck causing my breasts to press into him involuntarily. He brings his head down and bites each nipple through my t-shirt making me gasp.

"Later, baby, I'm going to fuck you until you shatter," holy shit, the angry Marco is so hot! He slides his hand down my panties, over my clit and inserts a finger deep inside me, palming my whole sex as he does. My hips move against his hand automatically. He removes it and pulls me off him and slaps my ass gently. "Now go or I won't be able to wait."

I start to walk off and turn to look at him playfully over my shoulder.

"Maybe I don't want you to."

"I *know* you don't want me to," he smiles seductively as he sucks my juices off his finger.

I laugh at him stopping to pick up my phone

when I see a message alert. I freeze and Marco's immediately behind me.

"What is it?"

I hand him the phone.

I know you're with him, you fucking whore! I warned you and you didn't listen.

Moving his eyes to my face he sees the color has drained from me.

"He's here, I know he is. I don't know how or why but he is," I say quietly as a gurgling of apprehension begins to bubble inside of me. I'm immobile with the familiar feelings of fear seeping through my limbs freezing me to my spot.

Marco shoves the phone back at me.

"Good, let's get this done with once and for all." His voice is cold and hard, his jaw clenched and nostrils flaring. "Go take your shower, Elizabeth." He picks up his phone and calls someone as I leave the room.

Turning into a zombie I go to the bathroom and begin the robotic motions of my bathing rituals, completely out of body. Put the shampoo in my hair, scrub, rinse. Conditioner. Rinse. Put body wash on shower poof, scrub body, rinse. Take facial cleanser, put a little in palm then wash face, rinse. I think I'm in shock.

I dress not really paying any attention to what I'm putting on. Clothes, yes these are clothes and they're supposed to go on my body. As I stand staring blankly in the mirror I hear a voice that I recognize so I go in that direction. It's Marco. I stand in front of him but I don't really see him. I'm in a kind of bubble where I feel detached and removed from everything making it all feel so surreal.

He bends his head down to look me straight in the eyes, putting his hands on my shoulders.

"Everything's going to be ok, Elizabeth. Now, sit down on the couch and wait for me. I'm going to take a quick shower. Don't answer the door. AT ALL. Do you understand?" He is calm and in control.

I turn my gaze to look at his face but it's only a reaction moving towards his voice.

"Yes."

"Good, now sit, baby," he says gently as he leads me down to a sitting position.

I just sit there like a mute...waiting.

He leaves me alone and the memories begin to flash through my mind. The hands coming to my face, the feet kicking me, the knife. They are flickers of buried memories bursting to the surface. And with them comes the fear, the desperation, the pain as if it all just happened. I begin to shake so hard my teeth chatter.

I don't know how much time passes, it could be minutes or hours, when I hear the lock click on the front door and it opens. I don't turn my head. I don't have to because I know who it is.

"There's my *wife*," Santino's voice penetrates my fog. "Aren't you going to come and kiss your *husband* hello? It's been a long time, *baby*." The words send shivers down my spine and I cringe at the sickening sarcasm.

I hear his footsteps approaching and I still don't turn. I can't, I'm frozen. I can't speak, I can't move, I don't even know if I'm breathing.

"I told you I would come back for you, Elizabeth. And here you are fucking another man, you dirty whore." His voice is cold, flat and full of hate. It hits me like a blow and I begin to sob.

'Don't make him mad, don't make him mad, don't make him mad,' is all I can think over and over again just like before because I know what will follow.

"I'm sorry, Santino," I choke out. "Why did you come back?"

"Why?!" He laughs hard, straight from the belly. "Because you're my wife and I love you. Look at me, Elizabeth."

My eyes travel slowly up his body. He's in sneakers, jeans, a short sleeved white T and a tan sleeveless vest with a baseball cap. He still has his head bald the way I asked him to keep it. He's a tall man at 6' with a slightly larger build showing the lingering muscles he used to keep himself built up with. He has a natural tan complexion and striking features. But what is most apparent about him is his quietly overpowering presence.

"Why are you crying, *baby*?" I hate that sarcastic tone he uses with me.

And I feel rage building inside of me breaking me from my bubble. Anger is an extremely motivating emotion. The fury and resentment from all of the beatings and humiliations, the past few years of terrorism and isolation, it takes over me and I burst.

"Why am I crying? Are you fucking KIDDING ME?!" I scream at him.

He laughs condescendingly at me, "*You're* angry at *me?* Are *you* fucking kidding me? You're the one who's been whoring around, I waited for you all this time and you couldn't keep your fucking legs closed, you slut!"

"Shut up, Santino! You know it's been over for us a long time. You kept up playing your bullshit games and I didn't say anything. I paid you back everything you gave up when you came here so I don't want to hear you crying that same old 'poor me' song anymore about the money!"

His hands jerk me up from the couch squeezing my arms tightly.

"I should have cut yours and your piece of shit family's heads off when I said I would," he snarls at me his face almost touching mine.

"GET. YOUR. FUCKING. HANDS. OFF. HER. NOW!!!" Marco bellows from the bedroom door.

Santino turns slowly to him with a sadistic smile

on his face but doesn't let me go.

"Prince Charming is here, how nice," he says sardonically looking at Marco. Marco's standing in the doorway dripping in his jeans, rage pouring off of him, fists clenched at his sides and his head is bowed as if he's ready to attack. Santino turns back to me. "Tell me, Elizabeth, did you swallow his spunk, too, like the good little whore that you are?"

"Let me go and get the fuck out of here!!!"

I wriggle free of his iron hold on my arms. He grabs me again and pulls me to him, my back pressed hard against his chest, his arm is around my neck and his face by my ear whispering.

"Do you remember that knife you took me to buy? I could put it in your back and pull out your guts before you even knew it was in you, *baby*. Then I'll do it to your boyfriend. Is that what you want?" The whisper is so quiet only I can hear him.

My breath catches, my eyes go wide and my mouth opens making no sound.

Marco moves towards us.

"STOP MARCO, DON'T!" I shout.

He stops, his eyes widening knowing something is very wrong.

"You are going to jail for a very long time, Santino," Marco hisses at him.

"I don't think so, my friend." Santino's cockiness is sickening.

"The computer hacking, breaking and entering,

endangerment, the list is endless, Santino. Let her go and leave peacefully and end this here." Marco puts his hands out palms down as he's trying to reason with him. There is a look of fear mixed with rage in his eyes as if he knows Santino has something at my back and he's very afraid for me.

Santino's arm begins to tighten around my neck. My hands go up to his forearms grabbing at them trying to loosen the vicelike grip on my throat.

"I am not breaking and entering. She is my wife and I lived here. And I let myself in with my keys," he says with sick satisfaction. "And I don't know what you're talking about with the computer allegations."

His arm is getting tighter and more constraining around me. I dig my fingernails into him now, trying to claw him off. I turn my head to keep him from crushing my windpipe. Panic is rising in me and my vision gets blurry. No sound is coming from my mouth as I feel like I'm choking.

"ELIZABETH!!" I hear Marco's voice from far away as if in a dream and it's the last thing I hear. I feel calm relief spreading thickly through me. 'It's finally over and I'm free,' I think as peace comes over me before everything goes black.

'Why are there people yelling? Did something break, I heard a crash? Ow, my throat hurts.' All of these thoughts are swimming in my head as I slowly wake up feeling somehow dizzy and confused. When I open my eyes Marco is cradling me in his lap. He's got blood dripping from his lip and his cheek is red and swelling. My hand reaches up to wipe it gently away. I realize I'm lying on the floor of the living room with him sitting here holding me. I turn to look around and see there are two huge men holding Santino down. And Mr. Jones is standing in my kicked in door, eyes wide.

"Sshhh, baby, be still, everything's ok now." Marcos voice is gentle and soothing.

"Why are they holding Santino?" Mr. Jones yells.

And then it dawns on me.

"You! You've been calling him! Why would you do that?" I scream hysterically at him, ignoring the pain from my throat.

Mr. Jones has a completely confused expression on his face. "He asked me to keep an eye on you and let him know if anything unusual was happening."

"Do you have any idea of what *he's* done?! DO YOU?!!" I am yelling at him at the top of my lungs.

Two police officers come running in and quickly assess the scene pulling their guns. One comes over to us cautiously.

"Are you ok? Have you been hurt?"

What a fucking idiot. You can look at us and see we've been hurt. But I look at Santino and my heart breaks. Even after everything he's done I can't inflict anymore pain on him. I loved him with a passion that you only read about, one that you hope you're lucky to have once in a lifetime. I still love him, love like that never dies. And I believe deep in my heart that he loved me too. But we were not meant to be together in this lifetime, not with the demons that he carries within that torment him. I believe in reincarnation, maybe in the next lifetime we will come together again and finish what we started.

I rasp out, "I don't want to press charges." I know Santino sees that I don't hate him, I never could. I just want him to be happy and find peace.

The officer looks at me in total shock.

"Are you sure, Ma'am? It's very obvious something has happened here. If someone has hit you we have to arrest him."

No one has hit me. This time.

I look up into Marco's face, there's anger, then understanding. He can't blame me for my decision because he knows I can't hurt Santino like that, even if it might be the right thing to do.

"I'm sure. I just want this to be over and to have peace." I turn to look into Santino's eyes. He's looking back at me with disbelief, longing, and gratitude. "No more," I tell him quietly but firmly.

Santino nods in understanding and I see a flash of regret and pain in his eyes. And all I can think of is, 'How can he think we will ever be together, especially after this?' The two giants look to Marco and he nods. I see the bruises and red welts getting darker on Santino's face. They let him up and Santino walks slowly to us, looking me deep in my eyes. I wonder for a moment if its bullshit or true sadness there.

"I won't bother you again, Elizabeth. Just know that I love you and I can't believe you betrayed me."

He walks towards the door as the two good-looking giants step aside and he leaves without looking back. I don't know if I'll ever see him again, that lingering love inside me hopes I do, that part that ignored the knowledge our story was a tragedy right from the beginning. A love that fierce and intense was forbidden and was always doomed. I'm filled with a deep sadness. A sadness for a love broken, for two hearts breaking, for pain that will never be forgotten. Marco pulls me into his arms as the sobs rack my body.

"Ssshhh, baby, it's over, you don't have to worry anymore." He turns to the men in the room. "I'll be right back," and he leads me to the bedroom.

"Lay down, Elizabeth," he says softly. He gently takes my clothes off and pulls the blankets over me as all of the emotions pour out of my body through my tears and sobs. He lies down next to me holding me tight, rocking my body soothingly cooing in my ear. When it finally subsides he kisses me gently on the cheek.

"I'll be right back, baby. I'm going to get a cool towel for your eyes." He goes to the bathroom and comes back with a cool wet washcloth and more tissues.

"Close your eyes, love," placing it softly over them. It feels so good on my hot face.

"I'm going to go into the other room and straighten things out. I'll be right back, you stay here and rest." His tone is gentle but firm.

I take a deep breath and feel my muscles begin to unclench.

"Who are those two guys, Marco?" My words catch from my still gasping breath from sobbing.

"MMA fighters from the gym I work out at. Friends of mine," he answers while stroking my hair. Like having two beautiful MMA fighters bust in your door is normal. "I called them when you went to take a shower."

"Oh."

"Try to rest, baby. You need it."

"Ok. I will. Sounds like a good idea." Suddenly I feel completely exhausted.

He turns my face to him and kisses my mouth lightly.

"I'm going to go talk with everyone. I'll come and lie down with you in a little while. Are you ok?" He knows my grief is from more than the events we just went through, I can hear it in his voice. There's trepidation and a little uncertainty there making his brows furrow.

I nod and smile warmly at him reaching up to

stroke away the concern in those lines on his face and he relaxes under my touch. Yes, this is an end and a beginning.

"Put the towel on your eyes and relax. I'll be back soon, baby." And he leaves me with one more tender kiss. My sadness is pushed quietly away with warmth and devotion. This mysterious stranger came and pulled me from my isolation, filled me with life and hope and desire. My heart swells with happiness of the promise of new beginnings and how lucky I am to have been given a second chance at a love that comes along once in your life if you're lucky. We've all been set free, even Santino. And I silently send a prayer of thanks out to the universe.

He's not even out the door before sweet sleep envelopes me.

Chapter 10

Three hours later my groggy eyes begin to open. I don't want to wake up, the sleep feels so warm, so good and so velvety. But my chest and legs hurt with something that feels like a tree stump lying on top of them. My throat is aching and my body feels like it's been beaten up. My mind begins to clear and I feel Marco's body wrapped around me and his deep steady breathing next to me. I smile in the comfort of it, stirring just a fraction and he pulls me tight.

"Hi," he scratches out with his sleep filled voice.

I snuggle up closer to him. "Hi." The word comes out hoarse.

"Are you sure you're ok, Elizabeth?" His voice is heavy with concern.

I turn to face him. He is such a good and beautiful man it makes me glow brightly inside. I put my hand on his cheek and smile letting some of that brightness shine on him.

"I am now absolutely positively ok."

He looks into my eyes studying them, breathing out heavily.

"I understand why you did what you did, baby, but are you sure it was the right thing to do?"

I look off somewhere in the distance letting my thoughts drift.

"There has been so much pain and vindication. It's time for forgiveness and moving forward," I look back at him, "and it has to start somewhere, Marco. I have to forgive him and myself. Or no one will ever be free. So, yes, I'm sure it's the right thing to do. For everyone."

He looks at me for a moment before his lips curve up to one side in a crooked smile.

"You are amazing, Elizabeth." He pulls me close, stroking my hair and I hold him getting lost in him.

I pull back and look at him my eyes wide in confusion.

"My door is wide open! We can't be in here with it like that."

He laughs out loud.

"Relax, it's already taken care of. Brian and John went home to get their tools and went and bought some trim and paint. They've already gotten it fixed and painted. It's good as new, baby," he reassures me pulling me back to him, kissing my forehead.

"Wow, those two guys are pretty good friends to have. I have to repay them." I say relaxing back in the comfort of his arms not wanting to leave.

"Don't even think about it. They are very good guys and would get insulted if you even brought it up. And I've already taken care of things with them."

I look up at him again with one more question.

"And what about Mr. Jones?"

A look of distaste crosses his face.

"I spoke with him a little as well but that is something you might want to address yourself, Elizabeth. I did let it be known that he was treading in waters of invasion of privacy. He acted like he was a little insulted but also a little scared."

I let out a heavy breath feeling content in the aftermath of the storm. We sit quietly each of us deep in our own thoughts as we trail feather light caresses over each other's skin feeling like this is right where we're supposed to be.

"What do you feel like doing today, Elizabeth? You've been through a lot." He's holding me with his chin resting on the top of my head.

"Exactly this, just being with you."

And that is just what we do.

Chapter 11

Sunday morning I'm dreaming the most sensual thing, it has me moaning and writhing and I feel my climax building. My orgasm wakes me to Marco's head between my legs licking me, tonguing me, filling me with his finger. The orgasm is intense, and thick like an opium high, somewhere between sleep and awake state. When I come down from my ride into bliss I return the favor, taking his engorged throbbing shaft deep in my mouth and suck every last drop from him.

Afterwards as we sit at the breakfast bar and I'm having my tea while he's making us breakfast I think I've got to be the luckiest girl in the world. I must have done something really great sometime to have Marco come into my life.

"What do you think about looking at some places I've narrowed down to the ones I'm most interested in moving to? I'd like your opinion on the locations and the layouts." He's in his boxers dishing the spinach omelets onto our plates. Sitting next to me,

I steal a forkful from his plate and his fork comes down grabbing a mouthful from mine.

"Are you kidding me? You're the real estate developer. This is your thing."

He bows his head laughing and says, "I still want your opinion."

Trying not to choke on a mouthful of spinach omelet I say, "Ok, it would be fun."

He smiles a huge grin with twinkly eyes. "Great, I'll call the real estate agent so she can schedule the viewings today." I see a hint of that naughty little boy he must have been as a child looking like he's up to something.

"Ok, I'll take a shower and get ready."

It's an absolutely beautiful day, almost eighty degrees, clear skies, seagulls flying above and a light soft breeze. It's always calmest after a storm. I decided on a pair of denim shorts, a long sleeve white jersey top that hangs off one shoulder and ankle boots. Marcos dressed in jeans, a white body fitting T which looks like it should be illegal on him and tan driving shoes. An hour and a half later we're meeting the agent at the first location. When we arrive she is professional but I can tell she would have preferred being alone with the delectable Mr. Marco Kastanopoulis, her eyes can't help but peruse his body. She is an impeccably dressed beautiful blonde southern debutante. Why couldn't he have had some portly older man instead of this Venus de Milo?

"Good afternoon, Marco. Thank you for calling," she extends her perfectly manicured hand to him.

"Hi, Brooke, thank you for agreeing to meet us on such short notice." Marco shakes her hand.

"Of course, anything for you," she replies flashing her bleached white teeth sweetly at him.

Bitch.

"This is my girlfriend Elizabeth DiStefano." He never breaks contact with my body showing his possession of me. I adore this guy.

"Nice to meet you, Elizabeth, I'm Brooke Williamson." She turns to me with a polite smile to shake my hand. I can't blame her for wanting Marco, she's not dead.

"Hi Brooke, thank you for taking time out of your Sunday, we sincerely appreciate it," I say to her equally pleasant.

She takes us to the first unit which is a downtown top floor two bedroom, two bath loft apartment overlooking the river, not too far from my place. It is lovely. Of course, it's an historic commercial building which was perfectly redone. The original bricks were left exposed along with the rafters and brushed glass was used in the main living area as partitions. The marriage of modern and traditional is beautifully done throughout the space.

I look at him, impressed. "Nice place."

He smiles back at me, "Told you, baby, it's like art."

The second location is a cottage in the Frank Lloyd Wright style, also in the historic district. It's quaint with the original stained glass windows and the dark woodwork gives it a masculine feel. Its two stories with two bedrooms and two baths with the original hardwood floors throughout and a small yard surrounded by black ironwork fencing.

The third unit is further out on the outskirts of Wilmington in the upscale Mayfair community. It's nice but what makes it appealing is the area. The homes are condos above the trendy boutiques and restaurants and there is a movie theater, gym and a popular grocery store on property. The community is very large and high end.

Our tours of all the locations are finished and we stand talking on a street corner in Mayfair, the end of season tourists and shoppers passing us by.

"Thank you again, Brooke. I'll call you and let you know what we've decided, maybe today or tomorrow." Marco turns to her shaking her hand again.

She takes it with both of hers and I'm thinking, 'Oh, no you didn't!'

"I look forward to it. Just to let you know, all of the homes are available to move in immediately. I know that was a concern of yours," she answers Marco sweetly.

He looks to me, ignoring her show of familiarity,

and answers, "Yes, that's perfect. Talk to you soon."

She leaves us and Marco takes me in his arms.

"I think she likes you, Mr. Bond."

He has the decency to look embarrassed, smiling sheepishly and blushing. "It doesn't matter, I just needed someone to show me some places. I'm with the woman I want to be with. Shall we go have lunch and talk about them?"

"Sounds good. Do you want to eat here?" I tilt my head to one side looking up into his gorgeous face feeling completely at ease.

"Actually I'd rather go back downtown. Pick a place." I can feel how relaxed his body seems against mine but he looks as if he's got something up his sleeve so I decide to go along with it.

"Sure. Hmmm," I look up as if I'm thinking hard, "how about the Riverboat Landing downtown? If the weather stays like this we can sit outside at a balcony table." There are private balconies with tables overlooking Water St., one of the few streets still having its original cobble stones.

"Excellent choice, Miss DiStefano." He puts his arm around me and we head back to the car getting glances from the passersby. I know they're not looking at me. I smile thinking, 'That's right, he's mine,' as a shiver of anticipation runs through me imagining being alone with him later.

The wrought iron balconies at Riverboat Landing are small and intimate only accommodating a small two chair bistro style table. You can have the sense of floating over the street if the glass door to the dining room is closed giving the diners complete privacy and seclusion. We're sitting at our table with our beers, waiting for our food to arrive when Marco asks me, "So, which place did you like the best?" I love how relaxed he finally is and I'm so grateful I have no more secrets between us.

I smile, really to myself, and say, "I think the first loft apartment really suited you." I can picture him in the sleek modern kitchen in his boxers making breakfast and being right at home.

"I want to know which one you like, Elizabeth." He leans forward and takes my hand and looks directly in my eyes. "I hope that you will move in with me. And don't say that it is too soon," he can see the surprise on my face, "because we both know that it's the right thing. And to be frank I want it now especially after what just happened. It doesn't have to be tomorrow...but soon." So, which place feels like home...for us?"

I sit back crossing my arms in front of my chest as annoyance begins to rise in me.

"I don't need your pity Marco."

"Don't insult me by saying that, Elizabeth. I have been trying to break down your walls since the night I met you. There is nothing standing between holding us back now." His expression becomes serious as if he's contemplating a problem that needs to be solved and continues, "There are, I'm sure....aspects of our personalities that both of us are not completely...familiar with yet but now that we have this behind us we can feel more...open and comfortable. So don't be so stubborn anymore and tell me which one you like. I have a feeling it's the same one I think." He doesn't rise to my unintentional bait by setting me straight and not letting me ruin the mood. This is why I love him.

I study his face seeing the sincerity of his emotions mixed with a hint of something else...maybe that secret I've felt that he's kept from me, that part of himself he's kept guarded. We look at each other, reading our expressions, he's determined not to back down while I'm fighting with old demons. I know without a doubt that I can completely trust him, I feel safe with him but I know there's a lot more to him than what's on the surface. What I have to do now is decide if I'm ready to walk through this door because I know with everything in me that it's a lot more than I've imagined.

Finally, I say quietly, "The first one."

He stands, leans over the table taking my face in his hands and kisses me deeply. "Me too," he whispers.

That night as we are luxuriating in the bath water that is beginning to chill, Marco says quietly in my ear, "Baby, I've arranged for you to have a court date on Tuesday to finalize your divorce. Don't argue with me. It's moving forward, love."

I move slowly to the other side of the tub and rest my back against it, my arms lying on the sides and my breasts on the surface of the water as it laps against my nipples. I place one foot gently on Marco's chest peering at him through lowered lashes.

"You know, it amazes me that one as confident, sexy and in control as yourself should even have to question my position, Marco," I say huskily. I slide my foot down his chest to his abdomen.

"Miss DiStefano, don't ever underestimate my knowing exactly how you are feeling, what you are thinking, and what exactly it is that you need. That would be a huge error on your part." His voice is gravelly, his hands gliding over my foot, up my calf to my thigh.

"I do not doubt that in the least, Mr. Bond, and it is precisely that I'm counting on." My foot slides down to press against his raging hard-on. "Now take me to bed and do what I need." I feel his cock twitch under my foot as his lips curve up seductively.

"Your wish is my command, Miss DiStefano," and he pulls my foot to his mouth and bites each toe then runs his tongue along my arch.

I push my breasts out wanting that tongue on my aching nipples, sucking in a deep breath.

"If you don't hurry, sir, I'm going to take care of this need right here," and I reach my hand down between my legs.

He grabs it stopping me, "Oh, no baby, I'm going to tease you until you beg me to let you cum. And I'm going to love every minute of it." His smile is wicked, curving the corners of those delicious lips. I have to taste them now.

I move fast, splashing the water over the sides of the tub, I'm on top of him sucking his lips into mouth fiercely, shoving my tongue so far down his throat, his face in my hands as his tongue rams down mine as well. I'm rubbing my sex hard on his torso needing the friction as my walls are grasping to feel him inside of me, filling me.

"Please, Marco, I want you now," I gasp.

His mouth clamps down on my nipple and a primal growl comes from deep within him. What we are doing is animalistic, a hunger so strong it can't be stopped. With his hands on my hips he slams me down on his cock and plunges in deep.

"Ooooooohhhh, yes," moaning I throw my head back, that's what I want.

I am a junkie and he is my fix. I feel the high seeping through every fiber of my being, carrying me into oblivion.

My head is back, my back arching and I'm riding him, my clit against his pelvis screaming out. I meet him thrust for thrust as the water splashes around us furiously with our movements.

"Yes, yes, yes, Marco! Please more!"

"Fuck me, Elizabeth, you feel so fucking good!" This sophisticated man and his dirty mouth takes me to places I only imagined.

I feel the orgasm ready to explode. He knows it too, feeling it.

He grabs my hips and grinds me back and forth on his cock, rubbing my pulsing tiny bundle of sensations up and down him.

"Cum, baby, I want to hear you scream." His head lowers and he pulls my nipple between his teeth and lip, flicking the tip with his tongue.

I shatter screaming as I dig my nails into his shoulders, rotating between grinding against him and slamming up and down on him. It's so intense. He's thrusting into me as his fingers press tightly into my sides, pounding me down hard on his throbbing cock, rotating my hips round and round teasing that bundle that's my clit. He jerks his hips and buries himself deeper inside me.

"Fuck, Elizabeth! Oh, God, baby," I feel him cumming and it intensifies my spasms.

Letting the aftershocks carry us down we lie still, breathing heavy, arms and legs entwined.

"Maybe we should get out now, Marco," I whisper. "The water is cold and we're all wrinkled."

He laughs, "Yeah, I guess," and he lifts my hips, releasing his semi-hard cock from me and my still pulsing sex clenches in protest. He reaches a hand down and washes his dripping cum from me while fondling my lips. Kissing me, he gets out to retrieve towels for us and one to wipe the water off the floor with.

"Wow, I'm surprised there's any left in here."

He looks up at me from the floor smiling sinfully.

"That was so hot, baby. You are incredible."

I blush profusely. "You've awakened my beast, Marco. She can't get enough of you."

He stands, still semi-hard, throwing the used towel from the floor to the side and grabs a fresh one. His look is hungry as he takes a step towards me. He holds the towel open beckoning me to step into it.

"Then let's go quench her need, love. My animal is hungry and wants to eat."

A shiver of warm desire heats me as I step into his embrace.

He leads me to the bedroom and takes two steps away from me. His eyes are dark and his cock is hard.

"Drop the towel." The commanding Marco is back.

The towel falls.

"Turn around and go to the center of the bed, baby."

I do, crawling, giving him a perfect view of my open sex and ass as my breasts sway side to side.

"Lay down for me, Elizabeth. Let me look at how beautiful you are."

I lie on my back and my body can't help but react to his intense look as it sweeps over me like a caress. He's fully hard again, flushed red with blood pumping through him.

"Stretch your arms over your head. I want to see those beautiful breasts reach for me."

My hands reach above my head and grasp the air needing to fill them with him. He walks slowly to me and bends down kissing me deeply. Lifting his mouth from mine he begins a trail of sucking kisses down to my nipples taking each one in his mouth as his hand slides up my inner thighs and traces circles around my clit. He lifts his mouth to my ear and whispers, "Where are your stockings, Elizabeth? I want to blindfold you."

My breath comes faster in wild anticipation of the intense sensations that statement brings. I'm like a Pavlovian dog, the word stockings immediately turns me on.

"In the top drawer," I answer quietly. I bite my lip as I watch his graceful movements. The dragon on his back is moving getting ready to go in for the kill. I can't wait.

He comes back with the stocking fed between his two outstretched hands, his expression serious. He joins me in the center of the bed straddling me, his erection so close to me I want to lower my mouth on it and swallow him.

"Lift your head for me a little, baby."

My eyes don't leave him as I do.

"Keep your arms over your head and close your eyes, Elizabeth."

And it's all black. Instantly I feel the hint of a breeze made by his movements and the warmth of his body on my skin. The air is filled with the sounds of our heavy breathing and the scratch of nylon. The feeling of pressure around my face and head is so erotic.

His tongue is on my lips, tracing my open mouth as his fingers are tantalizing my nipple.

"I want you to ride the waves of sensations, baby. Get lost in it. I want to watch the bliss of your high on your face and body."

"Oh, God, Marco, please...," I moan.

"That's right, Elizabeth. I am going to get drunk on pleasing you completely."

I feel the bed shift as he gets up, followed by the soft sounds of his bare feet crossing the floor. My heart is racing and I feel the wetness oozing from my throbbing sex. Every nerve in my body is on fire. I begin to rub my thighs together arching my back trying to quench my hunger that has just intensified instantly. My mouth is slightly open and a soft plea escapes me.

"Do you have any idea how stunning you look right now, writhing in anticipated ecstasy waiting for me? I could sit and look at you forever like that.

Almost ready to cum, aren't you, baby? Fucking beautiful."

"Please, Marco...," I beg quietly.

I hear his soft laughter from across the room. Moments tick by as images of his beautiful body doing naughty things to me go through my mind. My body moves in reaction to my thoughts, I can't control it. My hands clench the sheets, my back arches, my knees part beckoning relief to come and satisfy me. Finally he says, "Be right back, baby."

I listen to his soft footsteps then the sound of the door clicking. A few minutes tick by as my anticipation heightens. Click. The sound of door again followed by his silent footsteps. Clink. The sound of glass being set down. Oh, God, what is he going to do?

And he begins the dance of intoxicating seduction with his mouth and hands and fingers over my entire body. His fingers are tweaking and pulling my nipples showering them with attention as if they are the only thing that exists. Then fiery cold comes down on my erect nipple followed by his wet hot mouth.

"Aaaaahhhh!" I push my back off the bed, arching into him.

The hot cold slides across my flesh, leaving a trail of water dripping down my skin. His mouth leaves and is replaced with his fingers plucking the nipple as the ice circles the other and touches the tip making it rock hard. His mouth consumes it sucking it deep, flicking it with his tongue. The cold fire is sliding down my stomach and I suck in a deep breath as he stops at my belly button. It leaves a puddle that drips over my sides making my skin pimple. He continues the trip with the ice over my mound and touches my clit with it. My legs are wide as my hips buck. I'm going to explode from the overload of stimulation. The ice slides over my wet lips then he pushes it inside of me. His mouth is on my sex tonguing my clit as his fingers are inside of me, curved and rubbing that delicious spot as his tongue trails across my skin.

"Oh, God!" I pant out heavily.

He turns me over and slides his cock across my wetness and I moan pushing into him. Lifting my hips, his tongue runs up my back as his hands slide up the insides of my thighs, one going over my ass, the other grasping my sex. His body is between my legs as he circles one finger covered with my juices teasing my back hole. I move my hips into him asking for more. Our panting fills my ears. He slides the finger slowly inside me, the tightness pulling him deeper. His cock is sliding over my mound, taking me higher as his finger is sliding in and out as he thrusts his wide length into me.

"Yes, yes, yes, please, more!" I scream, thrusting back onto him. He's lying across my back now moving his finger moves from my hole forward grasping my clit, holding me to him as he pounds into me. I shatter into a million pieces, soaring in ecstasy.

He grabs my hips with both hands, pulling me onto his twitching cock inside of me.

"Elizabeth..," he growls as he plunges in deep, slapping his balls against me, holding my ass against him and his release is long and hard. I love how his body tenses when he cums.

We collapse onto the bed, him buried inside my still spasming wetness. He pulls the stocking off my head and throws it aside turning my face to him and kisses me with the passion he was just fucking me with.

"I can't get enough of you, Elizabeth...," he breathes heavily against my neck.

"Good, I don't want you to, Marco." I'm shattered still reeling from the intense orgasm, basking in the heady afterglow. My eyelids are drooping and I can hardly stay awake. And the last thing I am aware of is Marco's heartbeat lulling me to sleep.

Chapter 12

Tuesday morning and I'm a nervous wreck. I have to be at the courthouse in a half hour for the divorce, thanks to Marco. I am so worried I'll see Santino there, afraid of the emotional turmoil I'll feel. Marco insists on coming with me and I'm silently grateful for his strong presence.

Yesterday was full of requirements needing to be done at my office because of the allegations made by Santino to my company. I had to fill out background check authorizations and take a lie detector test. I tried not to feel humiliated, knowing that it wasn't anything I'd done that I should be ashamed of. Still, it sucked.

I decided to wear my grey slacks and turtle neck with black heels. I wanted to be as bland as possible, really feeling like I just wanted to melt into the cracks and be done with all of this crap already. Marco looked gorgeous in a crisp white shirt and a tailored black suit. His appearance was screaming confidence and I held his arm as my pillar of strength.

Santino wasn't there and after sitting there a few hours it was over in five minutes. It was finished and the past was finally behind us. When we leave the courtroom Marco looks down at me smiling and squeezes my hand on his forearm.

"Feeling better, baby?" His relief is evident in his voice and his face shows it.

My smile is as big as the Cheshire Cats, "Yes, so much better, thank you, Marco."

"Don't thank me, Elizabeth," he says kissing me on the forehead. "It was just what needed to be done."

"Well, thank you anyway so be quiet."

He laughs at me, "You sound like a little girl."

"Your little girl."

His expression becomes serious, "You're damn your right mine. It's about time you admitted it."

I look into his eyes as we're walking across the marble floor of the courthouse lobby and I say softly, "I knew it from the minute you said to me, 'Let's go, Elizabeth'."

His eyes become intense. "Me too, baby."

We walk to his car and he holds the door open for me then walks around the front and gets in, turning the key in the ignition."

"Let's go get some lunch. And then I have to go back to the office. But tonight I want to take you to dinner and celebrate. How about The George,

6:00?"

"Sounds perfect."

He looks at me smiling seductively. "I want to give you the present I got you tonight."

He sees confusion turning to recollection crossing my face, it's obvious the gift he told me he'd bought me completely slipped my mind.

"I'd forgotten about that. I get my present tonight?" A wave of heated anticipation runs through me.

"Yep." And he leans over and plants a quick kiss on my lips not saying anything else but his wicked smile tells me so much. My mind begins to go through the checklist of possibilities of what it could be but nothing, I'm sure, comes up with the answer so I decide to just enjoy the thrill in waiting. He looks at me knowing what is going on in my head and smiles delighting in his little game. Then he pulls out of the parking lot into the lunchtime traffic without another word.

At 4:00 I get a call from Carol.

"Hi Elizabeth, how did it go today?"

I'd taken the day off because I didn't know how long we'd be in court. Carol had no idea what happened over the weekend so I go over the highlights of the events and todays courtroom finale.

"Everything went smoothly. When they finally

got to my case I was in and out of there in five minutes."

She laughs, "Yeah, it's always the waiting that's the worst. I'm glad that everything is finally over and you can move on with your life. I can't believe Santino just showed up at your place and let himself in. Thank God everyone is ok, and I think you did the right thing in not pressing charges."

That lump is threatening to choke me up again. "Listen Carol, thank you for everything. You don't know how your friendship has helped me through this."

"Aw honey, I didn't do anything. I wish I could have gotten you to do this a long time ago but I had no idea."

"I know. Anyway, Marco's taking me to The George tonight to celebrate."

"That man has it bad for you, girl. I hope he knows how lucky he is."

I laugh at that. "I'm the one who's lucky, he's unbelievable." In so many ways.

"Well, you two deserve each other. I'll see you in the morning. And all of your privileges have been restored. So be ready to bust your ass tomorrow. Have fun tonight, kiddo."

"Oh, I'm sure we will, thanks Carol, bye." We both giggle and hang up.

I have two hours before Marco will be here to pick me up. It's a celebration dinner and I'm so excited about my surprise tonight I want to wear something with a bit of impact. I go to my closet and open the doors to look for something that I think he'll like. My eyes stop at the red dress. It's perfect.

By the time he knocks on the door at 6:00 I'm freshly shaved, lotioned, perfumed and clad in sexy red and 'fuck me' shoes. My hair is down sweeping across my bare shoulders and back. The dress is a deep front plunging halter which makes me feel almost naked. I open the door to a very sexy Marco in navy slacks, a white silk cotton body fitting T and blazer. His gaze scans the length of my body and I can see the erection growing inside his pants causing my body to instantly heat up. He's carrying a little pink box with a pink ribbon around it. His eyes take in the sight of my hardened nipples and a seductive smile curves his lips as he pushes the door open further stepping inside. He's standing so close to me we're almost touching. Closing the door without turning, he peers down into my face.

"I brought your present, Elizabeth," his smile is wicked.

I am one giant sexual nerve ending turned on by just his look.

"May I open it?" I breathe out soft and raspy.

"Of course, but I'm going to be the one playing with them." His voice is low and husky.

He holds the box to me and I take it tentatively untying the ribbon and hand it to him. My hands are shaking in anticipation. I pull the lid from the box and nestle it onto the bottom. My fingers gently pull the paper back. Inside is a pair of silver clamps attached by a silver chain. I run my finger along the cold metal and look up to Marco's face. He's smirking looking intently at me waiting for my reaction. Then he realizes I don't know what it is.

He raises his hand and flicks a finger back and forth against each of my pebbled nipples. Looking mischievously into my eyes he says, "They're nipple clamps, baby."

My mouth widens as I suck in a breath of air.

"I can't wait to see those beautiful pink nipples of yours in them, Elizabeth. It will make you feel like I'm constantly sucking, biting and pulling on them while I worship the rest of your body."

Oh, God, please just fuck me now.

The End.

Continue on Marco's and Elizabeth's journey in SWITCH....

SWITCH, part two of STRANGER

Elizabeth submitted to a night of abandonment with Marco, a complete stranger, after having lived in a self-imposed prison in fear of past threats coming to life. Their passion for each other drew them together pulling the past to the present and surviving it.

Now he promises to fulfill her every desire introducing her to a world of submission and domination with pleasures she hadn't realized she hungered for. She gives herself completely to him submerging herself in total erotic bliss. But can he submit when she wants to take control? And when the seductive woman who introduced Marco to domination comes back into his life can Marco stay away from her? Welcome to the world of power play.

About the story

I first 'met' Marco and Elizabeth four years ago when I wrote a short story of their first night together. They continued to pop in until I finally decided to write their full story. After **SWITCH** I will write Marco's back story and Elizabeth's and Santino's long story, it goes way, way back. I plan on telling you about Elsie's and Janie's upcoming love stories as well.

I am also working on a project called **MEMOIRS OF A YOUNGER MALE LOVER,** this is a compilation of short stories based on actual accounts of younger men and their more mature objects of affection. Currently this and **BOY TOY** are being considered for the title, message me on Facebook to let me know which you think you might like.

These are the immediate erotic pieces coming out soon.

About the author

N.M. lives on a secluded piece of property inland on the coast and loves to walk through town observing all the different types of people. She is addicted to reading and writing and wishes she was artistic so she could put pictures to some of her thoughts. She fluctuates between being a procrastinator and her OCD tendencies. Her children are her best friends and swears that if it weren't for them she'd never know the latest music, the radio always on high in the car as she sings when she's alone. And finally, she is a hopeless romantic with a dirty mind. Please join her on Facebook, user name N.m.catalanoauthor. She posts a lot of cool stuff.

9491293R00143

Printed in Great Britain
by Amazon.co.uk, Ltd.,
Marston Gate.